SOMEWHERE SANE

(A Piper Woods Mystery—Book 2)

Molly Black

Molly Black

Bestselling author Molly Black is author of the MAYA GRAY FBI suspense thriller series, comprising nine books (and counting); of the RYLIE WOLF FBI suspense thriller series, comprising six books; of the TAYLOR SAGE FBI suspense thriller series, comprising eight books; of the KATIE WINTER FBI suspense thriller series, comprising eleven books (and counting); of the RUBY HUNTER FBI suspense thriller series, comprising five books (and counting); of the CAITLIN DARE FBI suspense thriller series, comprising six books (and counting); of the REESE LINK mystery series, comprising six books (and counting); of the CLAIRE KING FBI suspense thriller series, comprising five books (and counting); and of the PIPER WOODS mystery series, comprising five books (and counting).

An avid reader and lifelong fan of the mystery and thriller genres, Molly loves to hear from you, so please feel free to visit www.mollyblackauthor.com to learn more and stay in touch.

Copyright © 2023 by Molly Black. All rights reserved. Except as permitted under the U.S. Copyright Act of 1976, no part of this publication may be reproduced, distributed or transmitted in any form or by any means, or stored in a database or retrieval system, without the prior permission of the author. This ebook is licensed for your personal enjoyment only. This ebook may not be re-sold or given away to other people. If you would like to share this book with another person, please purchase an additional copy for each recipient. If you're reading this book and did not purchase it, or it was not purchased for your use only, then please return it and purchase your own copy. Thank you for respecting the hard work of this author. This is a work of fiction. Names, characters, businesses, organizations, places, events, and incidents either are the product of the author's imagination or are used fictionally. Any resemblance to actual persons, living or dead, is entirely coincidental. Jacket image Copyright andreiuc88 used under license from Shutterstock.com.
ISBN: 978-1-0943-7943-2

BOOKS BY MOLLY BLACK

PIPER WOODS FBI SUSPENSE THRILLER
SOMEWHERE SAFE (Book #1)
SOMEWHERE SANE (Book #2)
SOMEWHERE WHOLE (Book #3)
SOMEWHERE FAR (Book #4)
SOMEWHERE WRONG (Book #5)

CAITLIN DARE FBI SUSPENSE THRILLER
COME GET ME (Book #1)
COME FIND ME (Book #2)
COME TAKE ME (Book #3)
COME CATCH ME (Book #4)
COME SAVE ME (Book #5)
COME STOP ME (Book #6)

MAYA GRAY MYSTERY SERIES
GIRL ONE: MURDER (Book #1)
GIRL TWO: TAKEN (Book #2)
GIRL THREE: TRAPPED (Book #3)
GIRL FOUR: LURED (Book #4)
GIRL FIVE: BOUND (Book #5)
GIRL SIX: FORSAKEN (Book #6)
GIRL SEVEN: CRAVED (Book #7)
GIRL EIGHT: HUNTED (Book #8)
GIRL NINE: GONE (Book #9)

RYLIE WOLF FBI SUSPENSE THRILLER
FOUND YOU (Book #1)
CAUGHT YOU (Book #2)
SEE YOU (Book #3)
WANT YOU (Book #4)
TAKE YOU (Book #5)

DARE YOU (Book #6)

TAYLOR SAGE FBI SUSPENSE THRILLER
DON'T LOOK (Book #1)
DON'T BREATHE (Book #2)
DON'T RUN (Book #3)
DON'T FLINCH (Book #4)
DON'T REMEMBER (Book #5)
DON'T TELL (Book #6)

KATIE WINTER FBI SUSPENSE THRILLER
SAVE ME (Book #1)
REACH ME (Book #2)
HIDE ME (Book #3)
BELIEVE ME (Book #4)
HELP ME (Book #5)
FORGET ME (Book #6)
HOLD ME (Book #7)
PROTECT ME (Book #8)
REMEMBER ME (Book #9)
CATCH ME (Book #10)
WATCH ME (Book #11)

RUBY HUNTER FBI SUSPENSE THRILLER
IF I RUN (Book #1)
IF I TELL (Book #2)
IF I LIVE (Book #3)
IF I FORGET (Book #4)
IF I RETURN (Book #5)

CAITLIN DARE FBI SUSPENSE THRILLER
COME GET ME (Book #1)
COME FIND ME (Book #2)
COME TAKE ME (Book #3)
COME CATCH ME (Book #4)
COME SAVE ME (Book #5)

REESE LINK MYSTERY
BEYOND REASON (Book #1)

BEYOND REACH (Book #2)
BEYOND REPAIR (Book #3)
BEYOND DOUBT (Book #4)
BEYOND NORMAL (Book #5)
BEYOND HOPE (Book #6)

PROLOGUE

Laurel craned her neck to stare across the desert. Her pulse quickened. Was there a shadow moving toward her in the failing light? *It's just your imagination,* she thought. *Well, that and the weird herb that guy sold you.* She let out a giggle as she lay back against the roof of her van, and lifted her arm to study the beads of the worn turquoise bracelet dangling from her wrist, each bead a tiny world of unexplored beauty.

The herb she'd taken earlier hit much faster than she had anticipated. She felt as if she were floating in the air, dissociated from her body, and completely entranced by the beauty of the world around her. The sky was turning a deep shade of violet as the sun disappeared, and the stars flickered like distant fireflies. The Arizona desert sprawled out around her, an endless landscape of sand and cacti that stretched for miles in every direction. Its emptiness, space, and freedom called to her; there was something intoxicating about knowing that nobody in the world knew where she was—not her friends, not her parents. *Especially* not her parents.

"Finally free," she whispered, her voice barely audible against the howling wind. "No more rules, no more expectations."

As she ran the bracelet's beads through her fingers, Laurel recalled the moment her parents kicked her out of their house; their words rang in her ears. According to them, she had "disappointed" them by dropping out of school and by "falling in with the wrong crowd." They gave her a choice: she could return to school and stop spending time with the friends who were such a "bad influence" on her, or she could leave. Laurel had chosen the latter, and she'd never looked back.

As Laurel remembered that day, tears welled up in her eyes. Now, finally, she'd found what she'd longed for: freedom, a chance to start anew and make something of herself on her own terms. A thousand possibilities filled her mind as she lay beneath the stars., and the wind rippled through her hair like an embrace from nature itself. Her imagination ran wild as she thought about all the places she could explore, all the people she could meet, and all the things she could learn if only she dared to take a step outside her comfort zone.

It didn't matter that her parents had rejected her; she didn't have to prove anything to them. What mattered was her quest to find her real identity, not the version of herself that met her parents' expectations.

As she gazed upon the desolate beauty of the Arizona desert, she wondered if maybe, just maybe, she had found a place that would allow her to discover that identity, a place that would not force her to conform to some mold.

"Out here," she mused, "I can just be me, without anyone trying to tell me who I should be." The wind carried her words away.

Lost in thought, Laurel traced the outline of the turquoise beads with her thumb. Their cool surface grounded her to reality. Her new life was only just beginning, and she vowed never to let anyone hold her back again.

"Nobody knows I'm here," she said to the desert, feeling a sense of peace wash over her. "And that's exactly how I want it."

As the sun dipped below the horizon, casting its last orange glow across the vast expanse of the desert, Laurel shivered. The chill of the evening air was creeping up on her. She sat up, hugged herself, and glanced around, taking in the beauty of the barren landscape.

There was that shadow again, lurking in the distance.

"What is that? A cactus?" she murmured, betraying a hint of uncertainty as she squinted at the object. The shape seemed to shift ever so slightly, creeping closer, and a sense of unease began to gnaw at Laurel's insides.

"No," she whispered, trying to reassure herself. "It's not moving. I'm just tripping, that's all. It's just a hallucination, a trick of my mind."

She closed her eyes, trying to believe her own words. After only a few seconds, however, she found herself opening her eyes again, irresistibly drawn to the sight of that shape.

Could it be a coyote? A stray dog, maybe? Surely it couldn't be a *person*.

"Hey!" she called out; her voice resonated across the empty desert. "Who's there?"

There was no response. The figure drew closer, and its outline became more distinct, detaching itself from the surrounding darkness. It was too big to be a dog, and too upright. It had to be a human being after all.

But what would someone be doing way out in the desert? Were they lost? Had Laurel parked close to someone's camp without knowing it?

Maybe they need help, Laurel supposed, trying to think clearly through her drug-induced haze. She was about to ask if that might indeed be the case, but just then, she noticed an object in the figure's hand, swinging steadily at its side. The object caught the moonlight and reflected it.

A hatchet? Laurel wondered as a chill ravaged her body.

All at once, her fear bloomed into panic, and she scrambled for her phone, her fingers digging into her pocket. The phone, however, was not there—she must have left it in the van.

She laughed. Of course, she had left it in the van—that was the whole point of coming all the way out into the middle of the desert, wasn't it? To escape the world, go where nobody could find her?

As the weight of her isolation settled on her like a leaden weight, she turned her head to track the figure's progress. He—for now, she could see it was a man—had continued to advance while she searched for her phone, and he was now only a short distance away.

Laurel's fear intensified. She knew she had to do something, but what? Her mind raced with possibilities, each more desperate than the last.

"Stay back!" she shouted, her voice wavering. "I mean it!"

The man continued his steady approach, saying nothing, the hatchet swinging at his side. Desperation clawed at Laurel's insides like a trapped cat. She had to escape this nightmare, but how?

You wanted to be on your own, without your parents or anyone else to hold your hand. Well, here you are. Now what are you going to do?

"Please," she whispered, her voice barely audible above the rising wind. "Just leave me alone."

Still the man did not speak. His head was tipped back, his eyes—sharp, silvery points in the moonlight—intent on her face. Whatever his intentions, it was clear Laurel was at the center of them.

Realizing this stranger was not simply going to go away on his own, Laurel forced herself into action. She scrambled down from the roof of the van, her movements clumsy and uncoordinated due to the lingering effects of the drug. She needed to get to her phone and call for help—it was her only chance.

In her haste to descend the ladder, however, she lost her balance and slipped, and fell hard on her back. The wind was knocked out of her, leaving her breathless and dazed as she stared up at the darkening sky.

Get up, she urged herself, her chest heaving with each labored breath. *You have to move.*

Somehow, she managed to push through the pain and confusion, and hauled herself to her feet. Her head pounded mercilessly, and her breathing came in rapid, shallow gasps. Despite her disoriented state, she knew she had to reach the relative safety of her van. If she could just get inside and lock the door, she could call for help. Or, better yet, just drive away. Either way, she *had* to get inside the van. It was her only hope.

"Almost there," she muttered, staggering toward the door. Before she could reach it, however, a shadow slipped between her and the van. The man was holding a hatchet, just as she'd suspected; the blade gleamed wickedly in the growing darkness.

Laurel froze, transfixed by the sight. Never had she been so scared in all her life.

"It'll be easier if you don't struggle," the man said. He took a step toward her, and Laurel let him come, let him think she was so terrified that she couldn't even think straight. Then, when he came close enough to reach out and grab her if he so chose, she kicked his shin as hard as she could. The attack clearly surprised him because he bent forward and let out a howl of pain as she shoved past him.

Then she was at the door; and, with a trembling hand, yanked it open. She climbed inside, hardly daring to hope she had escaped, and reached back to close the door behind her. The hatchet slipped into the opening, causing the door to bounce open again.

"No!" she screamed, kicking at the man until the hatchet withdrew. Then she slammed the door shut again, and this time it clicked.

She was inside, and he was outside. She was safe—for the moment, anyway.

"Okay," she said aloud, breathing rapidly. "Think, Laurel, think!"

The phone—yes! There it was, sitting on the edge of the couch, its black surface beckoning to her. She snatched it up and dialed 9-1-1.

"Pick up, pick up," she muttered as she heard the distinct sound of footsteps moving along the outside of the vehicle. Realizing the man might enter through the driver's door, she raced to the front of the vehicle, climbing over the console on her belly as she clicked the lock down. The man, however, didn't seem to have any interest in the door. He was moving around to the hood of the van.

Suddenly aware that the phone wasn't ringing, Laurel looked at the screen. No signal—not one measly bar.

"Shit!" she screamed, and hurled the phone against the wall. She began to hyperventilate, and she ran her hands through her hair to try to calm herself. The solution was so simple—she should just drive away! She probably would have thought of it much sooner if not for the drug-induced fog covering her mind.

There was a wrenching sound as the man used his hatchet to disengage the lock on the van. Then, he wrenched the hood open, propped it up—and disguised what was happening behind it.

"What are you doing?" Laurel muttered, uneasy. "What the hell are you doing?"

She scrambled into the driver's seat, pulled the keys from her pocket, and shoved them into the ignition. The van rumbled to life. Before she could change gears, there was a sharp hissing sound from beneath the hood.

Not willing to waste another moment wondering what this creep was going to do, Laurel shifted into drive and hit the gas. The man slipped out of the way just in time to avoid being struck.

"Yes!" she cried, pumping her fist in the air as tears of gratitude rolled down her cheeks. She couldn't see past the upraised hood of the van, but she didn't care. She would drive and keep on driving until she saw some sign of civilization outside the window, and then she would get help.

She had only gone forty or fifty feet, however, when the van began to slow. The engine coughed… and then stalled.

"No, no, no!" she shouted, slamming her hand against the wheel. She tried starting it again, but it would not turn over.

He must have done something to it, she thought as her fear returned with full force. *He disabled it somehow.*

As the implications of this reality settled in, she heard a knock on the door of the van. Her blood went cold at the sound.

This can't be happening.

The knock came again, louder this time, more insistent.

Laurel turned to the console, searching for something she could use as a weapon. Chapstick? Sunglasses? A pen?

There was a gentle rapping sound on the window beside her. Dreading what she would see, she turned to the window. There he was, staring in at her, grinning. He pulled the hatchet back, like a wind-up toy ready to let go with full force.

Laurel screamed—the sound was swallowed up by the walls of the van, trapped there like a bottle dropped into the depths of the sea.

CHAPTER ONE

FBI Agent Piper Woods was crouched behind a snow-dusted bush, opening the lock-picking set with trembling hands. The biting cold of the North Dakota wilderness numbed her fingers as she inserted the tension wrench into the keyhole of the door, a door that led into the Havenwood Falls Ranger Station.

"Come on, Piper," she muttered to herself, struggling to calm her nerves. Breaking the law was not something she took lightly—she had, in fact, spent much of her life catching those who thought themselves above the law. And yet here she was, attempting to pick the lock of a national park service building. A crime she could be arrested for.

Despite the guilt gnawing at her insides, the prospect of finding information about her mother, whom she had believed to be dead for years, more than compensated for any worry about the consequences of her actions. She'd been only a little girl when her mother, an Inuit, left home to visit family in a nearby village, a trip from which Ila Woods had never returned. Piper's father, Luke, had insisted foul play was involved, but Piper had believed her father was simply being paranoid. Until that was Piper bumped into a park ranger who claimed to have spoken with a woman named Ila Woods about a year earlier. According to the ranger, Ila had been carrying delphinium flowers, which were highly toxic. Given Ila's extensive knowledge of flora, Piper knew her mother must have picked them on purpose. She had no doubt intended to be seen, too, since Ila could blend into the wilderness like a ghost when she wanted to.

So why had she shown up out of the blue with a handful of toxic wildflowers? Could it be she was sending Piper a message, maybe warning her about some danger?

Piper didn't know the answer, which was exactly why she had to break into this ranger station and access its records, looking for any reports that might hint at her mother's whereabouts—the discovery of an abandoned shelter, perhaps, or a hiker claiming to have seen a woman living in the park. Piper would have much preferred to simply ask for help and avoid all this trouble, but since she had been warned by her boss against using her authority as an FBI agent to investigate personal matters, she had little choice but to color outside the lines.

Besides, she needed to see the evidence for herself. There were too many signs a ranger might miss, too many key details someone who didn't know her mother might overlook. If she had to risk her reputation – and perhaps her freedom, as well – to find her mother, then so be it.

The frigid air of the early winter morning pierced her lungs as she glanced around at the surrounding landscape. Tall pines and spruce trees stood like silent guardians, their branches heavy with freshly fallen snow. In the distance, a lone coyote howled, its eerie cry echoing through the otherwise quiet forest. The desolate beauty of the wild was both captivating and unsettling. Ordinarily, it would have comforted Piper, but this morning it made her feel isolated and vulnerable.

She was not entirely alone, however. In the near-empty parking lot, a solitary vehicle – a beat-up pickup – sat covered in frost, its owner likely inside the ranger station. Piper knew she needed to work quickly before being discovered.

Focus, Piper, she told herself, steadying her hand as she maneuvered the rake pick into the lock. The metallic clicks and scrapes seemed unbearably loud in the stillness, making her wince with each movement.

As Piper worked the lock, she recalled those long hours at Quantico, honing her technique in lock picking as well as many other skills. The grueling training sessions had stretched her physical and mental limits, pushing her to excel in areas like hand-to-hand combat, firearms training, and crime scene analysis, continually finding herself underestimated by many of her male colleagues. She'd proved herself many times over, however, and now she tapped into that grit as she focused on her task.

"Got it," she whispered as the lock finally gave way with a satisfying click. Heart pounding, Piper slowly opened the door, careful not to make any noise. She stepped into the dimly lit ranger station, the scent of stale coffee and wood polish filling her nostrils.

She paused, straining her ears for any sound of life. The last thing she wanted was to run into someone on duty. As much as she needed to learn the truth about her mother, she would not harm another human being along the way. She would sooner surrender herself than hurt someone who was only doing their job.

Hearing nothing, she moved forward. Her thoughts raced as she moved cautiously through the hallways.

Think, Piper. Where would they keep the records?

She spotted an office door and hurried over to it. Taking a deep breath, she carefully pushed it open, revealing rows of file cabinets and a cluttered desk.

"Jackpot," she whispered, stepping inside. As she began her search, the adrenaline coursing through her veins only heightened her senses. Every creak of the floorboards, every distant rustle outside, sent a shiver down her spine.

Stay calm, she reminded herself, her fingers trembling as she rifled through the files. Time was running out, and she couldn't afford any mistakes now.

All of the files, however, were old, most of them going back twenty or more years. Where were the newer files?

She looked around, wondering what she was missing. Then she noticed the sleek computer monitor sitting on the ranger's desk, the dim light from the screen casting eerie shadows across the room.

Of course, they're on the computer! What do you think this is, the Stone Age?

Technology was not exactly her friend – that was one of the consequences of having "roughed it" for so many years with her father, who'd instinctively distrusted technology – and so she sometimes forgot how convenient it could be. She just hoped her limited technical skills would be enough to get her inside the computer.

She glanced around, making sure the coast was still clear. In the distance, the sound of water running reached her ears—apparently, the ranger was in the bathroom.

Timing was everything now.

She slid into the chair at the desk, her heart pounding like a drum. Her fingers danced across the keyboard, attempting to guess the password.

"Ranger123"—no luck.

"NorthDakota"—denied again.

With each failed attempt, her frustration grew.

Damn it, why didn't I pay more attention during those tech classes in Quantico? she thought, frustrated. Back then, she had been largely focused on honing her physical skills and proving that she belonged among the male-dominated ranks of the Bureau, but now she wished she had absorbed more of the technical knowledge as well.

"The password's got to be here somewhere," she whispered to herself as she began searching around the computer for a sticky note.

She checked the sides of the monitor, then began pulling open the desk drawers.

The sound of the bathroom door creaking open sent a jolt of panic through her, and she realized her time was running out. If the ranger came directly back to the office, he would discover her in seconds.

Hoping the ranger had other things to do (such as making a pot of coffee in the kitchen, for example), Piper opened the last drawer on the desk. There, stuck to the side, was a note with the name of the Wifi and the Wifi password. Below these were the login credentials for the computer.

There it is! she thought, quickly committing the details to memory. She was desperate to sit down and enter the information into the computer, but she knew there was no time. Better to sneak away and return than to get caught.

Hurrying out of the office, she managed to slip around the corner just as the ranger stepped into the hallway, whistling as he walked. She steadied her breathing, all the while making sure she didn't forget the login credentials she had memorized.

Please find something else to do, she thought. *Don't go back into the office.*

To her relief, she heard the ranger's footsteps pass the office. Now, however, he was heading directly toward *her*.

Anxious to find somewhere to hide, Piper spotted a nearby supply closet, the door standing ajar. She slipped inside and, wincing in anticipation of a telltale creak of the hinges, eased the door shut.

The hinges did not creak, and the ranger walked past her hiding spot without a second glance.

Then she heard the ranger's voice. She peeked out of the closet to see the ranger standing at the end of the hallway gazing out the window, his phone pressed to his ear—talking to his wife, by the sound of it.

It was just the distraction Piper needed. She crept back around the corner, heading toward the office. She was so eager to get inside and search the computer that she didn't hear the footsteps outside until they had already reached the door. The exterior door swung open just as Piper was crossing the hallway, and she found herself staring at the puzzled face of a large, bearded man in a ranger's uniform.

A *second* ranger.

"Who the hell are you?" he said.

CHAPTER TWO

Piper sat alone in the sterile, dimly lit interrogation room. The cold metal chair beneath her did nothing to ease her discomfort. She felt suffocated within the four oppressive walls that seemed to close in on her, trapping her like a cornered animal. The silence was deafening as she anxiously waited to hear her fate.

Despite the weight of guilt bearing down on her shoulders, she knew she'd broken into that ranger station for the best of reasons. How else was she to learn her mother's fate? *I'd do it again if given the chance,* she thought. Did this make her a fool? Should she have learned her lesson, or was it possible that her good intentions justified her unlawful actions?

The door creaked open, and Doug Maxwell, Piper's former FBI boss, stepped into the room. He was a tall, stoic man with a face that showed years of dedication to his work. Piper glanced up at him, and her eyes met his stern gaze. She felt her stomach twist into knots.

"Can I get you anything to drink?" Maxwell asked, breaking the silence. His voice held a hint of concern, though his expression remained unreadable.

"No, thank you," Piper muttered, her voice barely audible. She knew what was coming next, and she braced herself for the impact. The fact that Maxwell was here meant the Bureau was taking this matter very seriously.

"Alright then." Maxwell sighed, taking a seat across from her. "Piper, you've committed a federal crime. Illegally accessing the national park registry is no small offense, and if you're charged, there will be serious consequences." He paused, and his eyes softened ever so slightly. "I never thought I'd see you in a situation like this. You were one of my best agents for years, and it pains me to see you here."

Piper looked away; the weight of Maxwell's words only added to her guilt. She knew she had made a mistake, but she didn't know whether the mistake was in committing the crime or not being more careful so that she didn't get caught.

"I want to know why," Maxwell said. "What in the world were you thinking?"

Piper took a deep breath. Her hands trembled in her lap. She knew she had to explain her actions, no matter how futile it seemed at this point. "I broke into the ranger station because I needed information about my mother," she said, forcing herself to look Maxwell in the eye. "There was no legal way for me to access that information, and I felt… I felt like I had no choice."

Maxwell's eyes held a hint of sympathy, but he remained firm. "I understand why you did it, Piper. But the law is the law, and your actions have consequences." He leaned back in his chair and studied her intently before continuing. "However, there is one way I can help you out." He slid a case file across the table, its contents hidden from Piper's view.

Piper stared at the file. A mixture of hope and dread filled her chest. It felt as if the room were closing in on her; the cold metal table seemed to press against her wrists, and the stark white walls seemed to lean toward her, devoid of warmth or comfort. She understood what Maxwell was offering—a chance to return to the Bureau and avoid prosecution for her crime. But she had left the FBI for a reason, and she wasn't ready to go back.

Her gaze flicked between Maxwell and the case file, her heart pounding in her ears. She didn't reach for it. "You're asking me to come back to the Bureau," she said slowly, the words feeling like sandpaper against her throat. "You understand why I left, don't you?" She'd never really explained to Maxwell her reasons for leaving in detail, but everyone in her unit had seen how the death of Fiona Taylor had affected her. Maxwell had to know.

If Maxwell did understand how traumatic Fiona's death had been for Piper, however, he did not mention it.

"This is the only way you won't be prosecuted for breaking into that ranger station, Piper," he said softly, his tone leaving no room for negotiation. "It's the only lifeline you're going to get."

Piper's mind raced as she weighed her options. The thought of returning to the Bureau made her stomach churn, but the alternative—facing prosecution and possible prison time—was equally unpalatable. She clenched her hands into fists, her nails digging into her palms as she struggled to keep her emotions in check.

"Is there really no other option?" she whispered, her voice cracking under the weight of her decision. Maxwell's silence was answer enough.

The seconds ticked by, each heavier than the last. Piper stared at the cold steel table, her thoughts a whirlwind. She considered the possibility of just going to prison and serving her time. Maxwell's offer felt like blackmail, and it left a bitter taste in her mouth.

Just one year ago, Piper had been on the trail of Byron Gray, hellbent on bringing him to justice for his crimes and preventing him from victimizing any more women. The guilt of her failure to stop Gray—and to save Fiona—had burrowed deep inside her, gnawing away at her conscience. The thought of returning to a line of work where lives hung in the balance terrified her.

"Look, I know this is a difficult decision," Maxwell said, his voice softening. "But you need to think about what's best for you. Do you really want to spend the rest of your life shut up in a cabin in the middle of nowhere? Is that going to give your life meaning?"

Before Piper could respond, the door opened, and her former partner, Wade, stepped into the room. His large frame filled the doorway, his dark eyes meeting hers with a mix of concern and determination.

"Hey, Pip," he said softly, his lips pressed together in a regretful smile as if he wished they were meeting under different circumstances. He turned to Maxwell. "Mind if Agent Woods and I have a minute alone?"

Maxwell hesitated, looking surprised by this, and then he nodded and left the room, closing the door behind him.

Wade sat down and studied Piper from across the table, his eyes searching her face. He seemed to be waiting for something.

"I had to do it," she said.

"Had to break into a ranger station?" he asked, arching an eyebrow. "That's a new one."

She lowered her face into her hands, thoughts of Maxwell's offer swirling in her head. "It's about my mother, Wade."

"Your mother?" There was a note of surprise in Wade's voice. "Is this about what that ranger told you, the one who thought he might've seen her?"

Piper nodded, staring earnestly at her partner, willing him to understand. "It was the only way I could look for her—I couldn't exactly say I was on official FBI business, considering the fact that I haven't been reinstated. I needed that information, but there was no official channel for me to use to get it."

Wade shook his head, looking puzzled. "What information?"

"I don't know. Anything that might tell me where she is, or what she's been doing. I'm desperate, Wade."

Wade glanced away as if it hurt him to see Piper this vulnerable. He cleared his throat and shifted his feet.

"You should've told me," he said. "I would've tried to help me."

"You would've tried to convince me not to break into the station."

"And would that have been such a terrible thing?"

They both fell silent. As much as Piper wanted Wade to understand where she was coming from, there was no way to convey the emotional impact of discovering her long-lost mother might still be alive. He could only imagine what she was going through, and that wasn't the same thing—not by a long shot.

"Maxwell's blackmailing me into coming back to the Bureau," she said.

Wade leaned back in his chair and sighed. "Guess I shouldn't be surprised. He sure knows how to lever a difficult situation to his advantage."

"I'm trapped, Wade. If I don't do what he says, there could be charges. I could go to prison over this. Imagine me in prison—me, someone used to being alone and having miles and miles of wilderness to myself."

"You'd go crazy."

She nodded. "You need to talk to him, try to reason with him. I've done a lot for the Bureau—he shouldn't treat me this way." She felt her anger rising to the surface. She wasn't just angry at Maxwell but at herself, too, for getting herself into such a situation. She hated feeling so helpless.

Wade tapped his fingers slowly on the edge of the table, lost in thought. Then he said, "I know how you feel, Pip. But there's something else you should know." He leaned forward, elbows on the table, his gaze never leaving hers. "I want you to come back, too. I'm working on a case—a really difficult one—and I need your help."

Piper felt as if she'd been punched in the gut. How could Wade ask such a thing of her? He was her partner, the one person who was supposed to have her back—or had been, anyway. How many cases had they worked together? How many long nights sitting in cars and eating out of cartons? This was how he showed his loyalty, by ganging up on her and pressuring her to do something she didn't want to do?

Something that had traumatized her already and could easily do so again?

"Please, Pip," Wade implored, his voice cracking. "I wouldn't ask if I didn't believe it was important."

Piper stared at Wade, disbelief clouding her eyes. "You want me to come back? After everything I went through?" The hurt in her voice was palpable, and she felt a knot forming in her stomach. Betrayal wasn't something she had expected from him.

Wade sighed and rubbed the back of his neck, looking a bit shamed by her words. "I know it's hard, Pip, but hear me out. You're wasting your talents hiding away in that cabin in Alaska."

The mention of her secluded home brought forth memories of cold, lonely nights spent staring at the fire, trying to forget the faces of those she couldn't save. But she also remembered the peace she'd found there, far away from the chaos of her former job, far away from people who needed her to save them.

"This is what you were made for," Wade continued, his tone gentler now. "You have a gift for this work, and I think deep down, you'll never forgive yourself if you don't use it to help others."

Piper hesitated, her thoughts racing as she weighed his words against her own fears. She couldn't deny that she missed the adrenaline-pumping chases and late-night strategy sessions. And Wade was right; her guilt wouldn't disappear just because she hid from it.

"Plus," Wade added with a wry smile, "I've got to admit, I miss working with you."

She stared at him, and her earlier anger began to dissolve. Maybe he really did believe this was best for her, and he wasn't just leveraging the situation for his own ends. That wasn't the kind of man Wade was, anyway. He'd always looked out for her, always stood up for her. He wouldn't ask her to come back if he didn't think it was the right thing for her to do.

Piper was still absorbing Wade's words when the door swung open, and Maxwell reentered the room. He took a moment to look at both of them, his eyebrows raised expectantly.

"So?" he asked. "Have you made a decision, Piper?"

Her heart pounded in her chest, and she looked from Maxwell to Wade. It was Wade's expression that tipped the scales, the same look he'd given her countless times before—one of unwavering support and trust. She knew that he would stand behind her either way, and this freedom to do what she needed to do convinced her.

Piper swallowed the lump in her throat, then finally spoke. "Alright. If you can make the incident at the ranger station go away… I'll come back to the Bureau. I'll get back to work."

Maxwell nodded, looking satisfied, and Wade's eyes shone with relief and gratitude. Piper did her best to put on a brave face.

Inwardly, however, she wondered if she hadn't just made a terrible mistake.

CHAPTER THREE

Staring out the airplane window and watching the clouds drift lazily below her, Piper felt a tightening in her chest as she wondered if she had made the right decision in returning to the Bureau.

I ought to be out there looking for my mother, she thought. *She was sending me a message, and I need to figure out what it was.*

A fleeting image of her mother holding a bouquet of poisonous flowers flickered through her mind, and she found herself wondering for the millionth time why her mother had remained hidden all these years if she was indeed still alive. Had she abandoned Piper? Or was there some unknown danger lurking in the shadows, a danger that would surface if they were to make contact?

"Must be strange," Wade said from beside her in his deep, rumbling voice. "Traveling like this after so much time in one place."

Piper glanced over at her partner, taking in his large frame and the way his dark skin contrasted against the light blue fabric of the plane seat. His eyes held a warmth that always seemed to put her at ease, and she realized she had missed him over the past year. It was good to see him again.

"Yeah, it's odd," she agreed. "What about you? Been traveling a lot?"

"For work," he said with a shrug. "Always dreaming of that sandy beach, but don't get there very often."

Despite the innocence of this small talk, Piper sensed an undercurrent of unspoken romantic tension running beneath the conversation. It made their words feel weighted, every glance lingering a little too long.

Piper found herself inwardly questioning Wade's motivations for wanting her back on this case. Did he harbor feelings for her, or did he simply trust her skills as an investigator? And what about her own emotions? She'd been drawn to him previously when they worked together...but was that attraction still there? Or was she merely enjoying the company of a good-looking man who treated her well?

Their conversation was cut short by the arrival of a flight attendant, her practiced smile never faltering as she offered them drinks from a cart. "Coffee for me, please," Wade said.

"Tea," Piper said, at which Wade grinned as if enjoying how predictable this was.

The attendant nodded and continued down the aisle, leaving the agents alone with their thoughts. An awkward silence settled between them, heavy and tangible like a blanket draped over their shoulders. Piper fiddled with her cup, desperate to fill the void. She seized upon the one thing that had always brought them together—their work.

"So," she said suddenly, "what can you tell me about this case you so desperately needed my help on?"

Wade grunted. "Easy now. I think 'desperately' is a little extreme." There was a mischievous gleam in his eye, and Piper realized she'd missed his sense of humor, too.

"Then what word would you use?"

"'Urgently' might be a better word." His face grew serious, and he sighed deeply. "It's a double homicide in Arizona. Two young women were found strangled to death within twenty miles of one another—one last night, the other two nights ago. Neither of them lived in the area; they were visiting from out-of-state."

Piper's curiosity was piqued, and she crossed her arms, thinking. "Do we have any leads? Witnesses? Anything?"

"Unfortunately, there's not much." Wade ran a hand through his close-cropped hair, frustration etched on his face. "I was only put on the case last night."

"And how do we know these two killings are related?"

Wade paused, considering the question. "At this point, there's no definitive evidence that the murders are linked. But there are enough similarities that the most likely scenario is we're dealing with one killer. Both victims were female, about the same age, found in roughly the same area. Both were strangled, with no signs of sexual assault or other harm to the bodies. Given that we're just dealing with a few days here, it's hard to imagine the two killings aren't linked."

Piper nodded, tracking Wade's logic. "Any idea why these girls were in Arizona?" she asked, her brow furrowed in concentration.

Wade bent forward, unzipped the duffel bag at his feet, and pulled out a case file. "Not yet," he said, opening the file and scanning its contents. "The first victim, Brooke Armstrong, was found murdered outside the motel where she was staying. The second victim, Laurel

Higgins, was in her van—a sort of long term road trip, by the look of it. We'll know more after visiting the crime scene where the second body was found."

Piper nodded again, growing thoughtful. Another case. Already her mind hummed with possibilities as she tried to search for connections in what Wade had told her.

Piper clenched her jaw as a chilling idea came to her. She didn't know who was responsible for these murders, but given the short time frame of the two killings, there was a good chance his work wasn't finished.

He might have just begun.

* * *

Piper's sense of unease disappeared as the airplane's door opened, and she was struck by a wave of arid heat. She squinted against the harsh sun, taking in the vast expanse of red sand and scrubby vegetation stretching out before her. It was a stark contrast to the lush wilderness of Alaska, with its towering evergreens and crisp, cold air. Here, the desert seemed to swallow everything up in its unrelenting embrace.

"Welcome to Arizona," Wade said, stepping out onto the tarmac beside her. He took off his sunglasses and wiped the sweat from his brow with the back of his hand. "It sure beats the cold, if you ask me."

Piper studied the waves of heat shimmering above the ground. Beads of perspiration were already forming along her hairline.

"It's certainly different from what I'm used to," she said, unsure what to make of her new surroundings. She felt as if she'd been dropped on a foreign planet. She'd been to the southwest United States before, but after a solid year without leaving Alaska once, the change was jarring.

"Trust me, Pip, you'll get used to it," Wade assured her, slipping his sunglasses back on. Piper was not sure if she believed him, but she kept her doubts to herself.

As they made their way across the tarmac, Piper spotted a tall, spare man standing beside a dark Crown Vic. Sensing their approach, he straightened up and extended a hand.

"Agents Wade and Woods, I presume," he said, his face serious and unsmiling.

"That's right," Wade replied, shaking the detective's hand. "I'm Wade, this is Woods."

"Call me Piper," Piper said. "And you are?"

"Detective Jacob Snyder," the man said. "I've been working the Armstrong case from the start, and now this second murder, too." He took a deep breath and let it out slowly with an air of world-weariness. "It never stops, does it?"

"No, it doesn't," Piper said softly, wondering what toll this man's career had taken on him. There was a pause in the conversation, and she found herself getting impatient, eager to get started.

"Mind showing us to last night's crime scene?" she asked.

In answer, Snyder dug into his pocket and pulled out a set of keys, which he tossed toward them. Wade reached for it, but Piper leaned in front of him and snatched the keys out of the air, giving him a wink as she pocketed the keys.

"You can follow me there," Snyder said, gesturing at a pair of vehicles, a Crown Victoria and a black Suburban. "The Crown Vic's mine. The Suburban's yours for as long as you're in town."

"Sounds like a plan," Piper said. "Lead the way."

As she and Wade climbed into the Suburban, Piper shot a glance at the sun. It was high in the sky, and she suspected it wouldn't set for a number of hours.

She wondered, however, if those hours were all the time they had to work with before another body was found.

CHAPTER FOUR

As Piper steered the vehicle along the dusty road, she couldn't help but feel a pang of nostalgia for her Alaskan cabin. Everything here felt so open and exposed, unable to hide from the glare of the sun that beat mercilessly down from its lofty perch.

What would it be like to live out here, she wondered? *How do you even stay hydrated?*

Wade's arm stretched out, adjusting the dial on the AC. He was a big man, and he sweated easily, but even so, he didn't seem to mind the sweltering heat.

"You really prefer this over the cold?" she asked.

He pulled back as if stung by her words. "Are you kidding me? I might sweat like a pig, sure, but at least I don't have to worry about frostbite."

She shook her head, amused. "It's not that bad. You don't even get snow out here, and where's the fun in that? You're from Detroit, so I know you know what I'm talking about."

Wade's face grew serious. "That's exactly why I hate the cold so much. Mom worked three jobs just to feed me and my siblings, and there was never enough money to keep the heat going in the winter. We slept in our jackets."

He was silent a few moments longer, lost in thought. Then he shook his head as if to dispel the memories. "Anyway," he said, "that's what being cold reminds me of—poverty."

Listening to him, Piper was touched by the gravity and sorrow in his voice. She had heard him refer to his upbringing now and then when they used to work together, but rarely with such openness. She wanted to ask him more about this, but just then, he cleared his throat.

"Looks like we're here," he said, pointing ahead at Snyder's Crown Vic, which was parked beside a clump of sage bushes.

The dust from the unpaved road billowed around them as they pulled up behind Snyder's vehicle. All three of them stepped out into the oppressive heat, their boots crunching on the dry ground.

"Where's Laurel's van?" Piper asked, squinting against the sun's glare. As far as she could tell, this section of desert looked as featureless as all the rest of it.

"Already impounded," Snyder said, slipping his keys into his pocket. "Victim's body was removed last night, too, of course. Can't leave anything out for long in this heat."

Even though Piper had known the body wouldn't have been left exposed all morning to the desert sun, she was surprised nonetheless to find the area so empty. It was difficult to get her bearings or figure out where to begin.

Wade seemed to have a similar reaction. He raised an eyebrow as he surveyed the desolate landscape, a sea of sand and rocks stretching out before them. "So, who found the body?" he asked Snyder. "This place is damn near the middle of nowhere."

"Motorist," Snyder replied. "Taking pictures of the scenery when he spotted the van."

"Taking pictures of the scenery?" Piper asked. "Just a coincidence, then?"

Snyder hesitated as if he was reluctant to say anything. Then he sighed, resigning himself. "I thought the same thing, too," he said. "I pressured the guy a little, and he admitted he'd seen the victim earlier and was...smitten, shall we say. So he wasn't just looking around at random."

Piper was about to ask a follow-up question, but Snyder hastened to add, "He's not our guy, I can assure you. His hands are too small—don't match up with the bruises on the victim's neck. Besides, he had his two kids with him, and I'm pretty sure they would've noticed something."

Piper nodded, impressed by the legwork the detective had already done. "Thanks for getting us up to date," she said. "If you'll point out where the van was parked, Agent Wade and I would like to take a look around."

"Of course," Snyder said. He pointed to a patch of ground where Piper could faintly see the tracks of a vehicle, and she and Wade headed toward it.

Piper's first thought was to look for a second set of vehicle tracks. After several minutes of searching, however, neither she nor Wade came across any. She did, however, spot faint footprints in the sand, an elusive sign of human presence amidst the vast expanse of the desert. The sun glinted off her sunglasses as she followed the erratic trail, the indentation no more than ghostly whispers on the dunes.

After a short distance, the ground changed to a wind-scoured hardpan, and the tracks disappeared.

There were footfalls behind her as Wade approached. "Think they're the killer's tracks?" he asked, his large frame casting a welcome shadow against the relentless heat.

"Maybe," Piper said, frowning. "If so, I wonder where he came from."

Wade squinted at the horizon, his brow furrowing. "Could live nearby, maybe in a hut or something."

"Or he just parked further away to avoid detection," Piper said, her thoughts spinning like the dust devils dancing around them. "Either way, it doesn't look like he left us much of a trail to follow. These tracks just disappear into thin air."

Before they could explore the theory further, Snyder's voice cut through their conversation. "I have to head out," he called, sounding apologetic. "Need to take another look at that van—seems like the killer may have sabotaged the engine so the victim couldn't get away, then forced his way through the driver's window. Will you two be able to find your way back?"

"We'll manage," Piper said, smiling politely. "Thanks for your help."

Snyder waved and turned away.

The wind picked up, carrying with it a fine layer of sand that clung to Piper's skin and stung her eyes. She studied the area again, searching for any clues she might have missed before, but the desert refused to share its secrets.

"Maybe we should talk to the victims' families," Wade suggested. He wiped the sweat from his brow with the back of his hand. "See if they can shed some light on why they were out here."

Piper nodded, about to agree, when something on the ground caught her eye. She squatted down; her fingers brushed against the gritty sand as she picked up a small turquoise bead. She held it up. There were dark lines running across it, similar to the pattern sunlight made on the floor of a body of water.

Wade leaned in close. His brows furrowed as he examined the tiny object.

"Think it belonged to one of the victims?" he asked, rubbing his chin thoughtfully.

"Could be," Piper said, rolling the bead between her fingers. "Or maybe it was left behind by our killer."

"Either way, it's worth looking into. I'll make sure we get this to the lab for analysis. In the meantime, let's go talk to those families."

As they walked back to their rental vehicle, a sense of unease crept up on Piper. It was as if the vast emptiness of the desert was closing in around them, concealing secrets just beyond their reach.

Whoever this killer was, he seemed to know the desert well—which meant he could be anywhere, ready to strike when they were least expecting it.

CHAPTER FIVE

The hotel's elevator creaked upwards, dragging Lawrence Wade's stomach with it. He glanced at Piper out of the corner of his eye, tapping his foot to mask his nerves.

He hated delivering bad news, especially when he had to deliver it to grieving families. Hated it. Almost as much as he hated small spaces.

The elevator was little more than a metal box, all chrome and mirrors under flickering lights. As it climbed higher, his pulse quickened. He tugged at his collar, glanced at the floor indicator, and watched the numbers blink by. He wished they would speed up.

Piper leaned against the wall, apparently at ease. How did she stay so calm at a time like this? He rubbed the back of his neck, swallowing hard against the knot in his throat.

He thought of the grieving family members waiting for them upstairs. They already knew Brooke and Laurel were dead, but what they didn't know was that the police had no leads, and neither did the FBI. What they didn't know was that it could be a long, long time before they found closure.

They'll be chomping at the bit, demanding answers, he thought. *And what are we supposed to tell them? It's an active investigation, and we're pursuing all leads?*

This was the worst part of the job. Not the chase, not the danger, but delivering tragic news and reopening old wounds. He sighed, catching Piper's eye in the reflection.

"You're looking a bit pale," she said.

He grunted. "It would be nice to deliver good news for a change."

She pressed her lips together sympathetically. "I know the feeling."

The elevator shuddered to a stop. As the doors creaked open, Wade put on a mask of professional detachment. They had a job to do. No matter how much he dreaded it.

The hallway stretched before them, sterile and empty. Somewhere nearby, laughter filtered through an open door—children playing, blissfully unaware of the grief being felt just a few rooms away. Wade gritted his teeth and walked toward room 412, Piper at his side.

No use prolonging the inevitable.

He knocked sharply on the door, inwardly bracing himself. It swung open immediately, revealing a severe-looking woman with iron-gray hair, her eyes red and swollen.

"Mrs. Higgins?" Wade asked, a bit surprised by how quickly she had answered the door. She must have been lingering there, waiting for the agents' arrival.

The woman nodded and moved aside without a word, allowing the agents to enter. A man – Mr. Higgins, Wade supposed – sat motionless on the edge of one of the beds, staring at nothing. A younger woman – she had to be Felicity Armstrong, Brooke's older sister – slumped in an armchair, clutching her rounded belly as if it were a lifeline.

"I'm Agent Lawrence Wade," he said as he entered, "and this is my partner, Agent Piper Woods." He held up his badge for proof, then returned it to his belt. "We're very sorry for your loss."

Mrs. Higgins' face hardened. "Have you found who did this? Have you found the monster who killed my Laurel?" Her voice shook with rage and anguish.

"We're still investigating, ma'am," Wade said, trying to sound calm and reasonable. "We have some leads we're following up on, but it's still early in the case."

"You don't have any idea, do you?" Mrs. Higgins said, calling his bluff. "No idea at all!"

Felicity let out a soft, despairing moan, tears spilling down her cheeks. This was just the sort of thing Wade had been hoping to avoid—chaos.

"We understand you're upset," Piper said, "and you have every right to be. I promise we're doing everything we can to find the killer and bring them to justice."

Mrs. Higgins glared at her, unconvinced. Wade didn't blame Mrs. Higgins. If he were in her shoes, he wouldn't believe empty reassurances either.

"Have the accommodations here at least been acceptable?" Piper asked. It sounded like she was trying to change the subject, to direct the conversation toward more neutral territory, but she seemed unaware of how tone-deaf she sounded, and her clumsy attempt to defuse the tension backfired.

"I don't give a damn about the accommodations!" Mrs. Higgins cried. "I want my daughter back, do you understand me? I want my baby back!" She dissolved into angry, heart-wrenching sobs.

Mrs. Higgins' tears created a ripple effect. Mr. Higgins finally stirred. He rose to wrap his arms around his wife. Felicity cried harder, and clutched at her belly as if to protect the life inside.

Piper looked helplessly at Wade, clearly at a loss for how to handle this situation. Composing himself, Wade gave her a reassuring nod before addressing the others.

"I understand how devastating this is," he said softly. "No one should ever have to lose a child, and frankly, nothing we say can make it any better."

He paused. Everyone was listening, waiting to hear what he would say next.

"There's a lot we don't know," he said. "But that's why we're here: to ask you all about Brooke and Laurel. If anyone can help us fill in the blanks, it's all of you—if you're up for it, that is."

Piper shot him a grateful glance. Mr. Higgins guided his wife to an armchair and sat beside her, a solid presence of comfort. Felicity perched on the edge of the bed, clutching a tissue as fresh tears streamed down her cheeks.

Wade pulled up a chair across from Mr. and Mrs. Higgins. "When was the last time you spoke with Laurel?" he asked.

"Three days ago," Mrs. Higgins said dully. "She called to tell us she'd arrived in Phoenix safely. She was at some rinky-dink store looking at knick-knacks—Friendly Fred's, I think it was called." She made a derisive scoffing sound.

"Did she say why she was visiting Arizona?" Piper asked.

Mrs. Higgins hesitated. She bit her lip, her eyes darting to the side.

"What is it, Mrs. Higgins?" Wade asked, sensing there was something she was trying to avoid.

"Laurel…" Mrs. Higgins sighed. "We weren't on the best of terms with her, okay? We thought she was going through a faze – ignoring her homework, falling in with the wrong crowd, that kind of thing – so we decided what she needed was a little taste of the real world. We wanted her to understand how good she had it with us."

"We kicked her out," Mr. Higgins said despondently.

"We thought she'd come right back," Mrs. Higgins hastened to add. "As soon as her friends' hospitality ran out. But instead, she found this old van and started cruising the country, turning it into some kind of adventure. That's why we were so relieved when she called us. Even though she was still angry with us, she didn't want us to worry about her." She swallowed hard, her lips trembling.

That guilt must be tearing them apart, Wade thought, feeling sorry for these two. Their response to their daughter's behavior might have been a bit harsh, but they had never intended her any harm.

"Did Laurel have any enemies that you know of?" Wade asked. "Anyone who might have wanted to harm her?"

"No," Mrs. Higgins said. She looked up at him with red-rimmed eyes. "Laurel was kind to everyone. She didn't have an enemy in the world."

Wade nodded, not particularly surprised by this news. He turned to Felicity. "What about Brooke?" he asked. "Anyone from her past you felt you needed to keep an eye on?"

Felicity shook her head. "No one. It doesn't make sense why anyone would want to harm her. She was just starting fresh, heading out to LA for a singing gig she'd lined up. It was about the only thing she talked about when she called me two mornings ago."

"What about her behavior? Any surprising changes recently, any unusual moodiness? Did it seem like she was particularly stressed or anxious?"

Felicity shook her head again and let out a tired sigh. "Nothing like that. She was excited, eager to start her new life. The stars were aligning for her, you might say. If there was something wrong, she would have told me about it."

"Do you know if she was planning to visit any friends along the way?" Piper asked.

Felicity pressed her lips together regretfully. "Not that I'm aware of. I'm sorry, but that's all I can tell you."

Wade nodded, but his expression was grave. "Thank you for answering our questions," he said, rising from his chair. "Again, please accept our deepest condolences."

Felicity followed them to the door. "You have to find him," she said urgently, clutching his arm. "You have to find the monster who did this."

"We will," he promised, hoping it was a promise he could keep. Felicity stared into his eyes for a few seconds as if deciding whether or not to believe him, and then finally let go of his arm and turned away.

As the hotel door closed behind them, Wade and Piper walked down the dimly lit hallway in silence, the carpet muffling their footsteps. Wade breathed a pent-up sigh of relief, glad to have that conversation over.

When they reached the elevator, Piper let out a shaky breath. "Wasn't my finest moment, was it?" she asked.

Wade pressed the call button, and the doors slid open with a ding. Stepping inside, he gave her a sympathetic look. "It happens to the best of us. Just a brain fart, that's all."

Piper's cheeks flushed as the doors closed. She leaned against the rail, gazing up at the floor numbers above. "Guess living alone with nothing but wild animals for company doesn't exactly sharpen one's social skills. Go figure."

The doubt in Piper's voice caught Wade off guard. She had always been so confident and self-assured, so ready for anything. It was one of the many things he admired about her.

"Hey," he said, "everyone makes mistakes, okay? Don't beat yourself up."

"Too late for that."

The elevator came to a stop, and Wade put a hand on her shoulder. He felt the warmth of her skin through the thin blouse.

"You're a damn good agent, Pip," he said, looking into her eyes. "Don't ever doubt that."

A smile lit her face, and at that moment, he was struck by her beauty. His heart did a funny little flip as her eyes met his. He wondered if she felt the same spark that he did if there might be something more between them than just being partners.

The elevator door began to close, and Wade reached out to hold it for Piper. As he followed her out, he reminded himself that he needed to focus on the case.

He thought about the details the victims' families had shared with them and how little anyone knew about where the victims had been or what they had done around the time they were murdered. Anyone, that was, except the killer. Wade had a feeling the killer had studied the victims' movements carefully, fully aware that they were unfamiliar with the area and had no friends or relatives to look out for them. He had isolated them both: Laurel at her van in the desert, Brooke in her motel room.

Wade hoped that searching the motel where Brooke's body had been found would provide answers because until they got some concrete leads, the killer would be no easier to get their hands on than a ghost.

And there was no telling whom he might haunt next.

CHAPTER SIX

"Here it is," the manager said, pointing to a corner room on the ground floor. The door stood slightly ajar, yellow crime scene tape fluttering in the breeze. Piper's heart sank as she took in the details: the dusty footprints on the concrete, the haphazard arrangement of trash by the door, and the faint scent of bleach barely masked the odor of death.

Piper and Wade were at the Desert Oasis, the motel where Brooke Armstrong's body had been found. The manager, a young man named Luke with a pencil mustache and a nervous energy that seemed to radiate out from him in waves, stood nearby, shifting his weight uncomfortably as if hoping they would dismiss him soon.

"Can you tell us anything about the night Brooke was killed?" Piper asked, her eyes not leaving the crime scene.

"Um, well, she checked in around seven pm," Luke stammered, glancing nervously at Wade's imposing figure. "She didn't say much, just signed the register and took her key. I didn't see her again after that, but, uh, one of the other guests said they heard a commotion later that night."

"Commotion?" Piper repeated, narrowing her eyes.

"Y-yeah, like a struggle maybe? But it stopped pretty quickly, so they didn't think much of it until… well, you know…" he trailed off, swallowing hard.

"Thank you, Luke," Piper said, dismissing him with a nod. She stepped past the crime scene tape and into the room, Wade following close behind.

The room was small and dimly lit, a single window providing their only source of natural light. The bed had been stripped, its linens long since removed as evidence. The bedside lamp lay on the floor; the bulb was smashed.

"Look at this," Wade called from the bathroom, gesturing to a series of faint scratches on the tile floor. Piper joined him and examined them carefully, noting their direction and depth.

"Could be from Brooke's nails as she struggled," she speculated, her mind automatically cataloging the information. "He might've come through the window, then attacked her and dragged her outside."

"Why would he drag her outside?"

She frowned, thinking. "Maybe he was taking her somewhere. Or maybe he just preferred to leave her body in the open air." She shrugged. "The fact is, we know very little about this guy at this point."

Wade seemed to sense her impatience. "Let's go over everything again," he suggested. "Maybe we missed something."

"Alright," Piper agreed, taking a deep breath. Together, they combed through the room once more, searching for any clue that might lead them closer to the truth.

As they worked, Piper felt a powerful sense of empathy toward Brooke. She could imagine Brooke's terror, her confusion as she tried to grapple with the reality of what was happening. But even though Piper had been in a number of terrifying situations in her own life, she'd never experienced anything quite like what Brooke must have gone through.

"Find anything?" she asked, looking up from the carpet where she'd been examining a small stain.

"Nothing new," Wade said, his voice heavy with disappointment. "Maybe we should head out back to where the body was discovered."

The sun cast a harsh glare over the desert landscape as Piper and Wade stepped outside the motel room. The ground beneath their feet was a mix of cracked earth and sparse patches of brittle grass struggling to survive in the arid climate. A sense of desolation hung heavy in the air, only magnified by the silence that enveloped them.

"Looks like she was found right here," Piper said, pointing to a small area close to the dumpsters roped off by caution tape. "He must've dragged her out, then killed her here."

"Think he was parked back here?" Wade suggested. "Could've been dragging her to his car, then got spooked and left her."

Piper squinted against the sunlight as she surveyed the vast expanse of sand and scrub that extended beyond the motel. "Or he came on foot from the desert like he did when he attacked Laurel. It's possible the desert is familiar to him, a home of sorts."

"Like he's a survivalist or something?" Wade asked, wiping sweat from his brow with the back of his hand. His gaze lingered on the horizon as though he could discern some hidden truth in the endless expanse of sand and sky.

"Maybe," Piper said, her mind racing with the implications of such a theory. The idea that the killer might be someone who thrived in these harsh conditions, just like herself, sent a chill down her spine, despite the oppressive heat.

"But we can't know for sure until we find more evidence," she added.

"True," Wade said, his large frame casting a long shadow across the parched earth as he turned to face her. "So, if the killer did come from the desert, how would he have approached? There's not much cover out there."

"From what I can see, there's a small ridge over there." Piper pointed to the east, where the land rose slightly before sloping back down toward the motel. "It's not much, but it would provide some concealment if someone were trying to approach undetected."

"Good eye, Pip," Wade said, nodding in approval. He took a swig from his water bottle and wiped his mouth with the back of his hand.

Neither of them spoke. Piper tried to imagine what kind of person they were dealing with and where he might be now. At home, recovering from his night of hunting—and preparing to strike again?

Wade cleared his throat. "Come on, we should check out Brooke's vehicle. There's no telling what we might find."

The sun was a merciless orb in the sky, casting its scorching rays upon the desert landscape as Piper and Wade approached Brooke Armstrong's abandoned car. The rust-colored dust clung to the vehicle as though it were a shroud, concealing whatever secrets lay within.

Piper and Wade moved to opposite sides of the car, and together they began to comb through the vehicle's interior, which was dusty because one of the windows had been left partly open. The air inside the car was stifling. Piper could feel the oppressive heat bearing down on her, but she pushed the discomfort aside, focusing instead on the task at hand.

"Here," she called out, retrieving a crumpled map from the glove compartment. "Looks like Brooke had her whole route to LA mapped out just in case her GPS failed. Clever girl. Guess I'm not the only one who distrust technology."

"Good find," Wade said, his fingers deftly working to remove the car's center console. "Let's keep searching."

As they continued their examination of the vehicle, Piper couldn't help but feel a strange connection to Brooke. Though they had never met, she felt as though their lives were somehow intertwined—two women whose paths had crossed in the most tragic of circumstances.

"Check this out," Wade announced, holding up a small leather notebook. "It was hidden under the passenger seat. Looks like some kind of journal."

Piper took the notebook from him, carefully turning the pages as she scanned its contents. There, amidst the hastily scribbled entries and smudged ink, was evidence of Brooke's final days: her hopes, her fears, her need for a new start—all laid bare on the worn pages of her diary.

"Does it say anything about anyone she might have run into out here?" Wade asked, watching Piper's face closely for any sign of a breakthrough.

"Nothing," she replied, her heart heavy with disappointment. "It doesn't look like there's anything–" She stopped abruptly, her breath catching in her throat.

"What?" Wade asked impatiently. "What did you find?"

"She went to Friendly Fred's the day she was killed," she said softly. "The same store Laurel Higgins stopped at."

CHAPTER SEVEN

Piper shielded her eyes as she stepped out of the car, a feeling of unease creeping up her spine as she studied the small mom-and-pop store. Friendly Fred's seemed almost too perfect, like a mirage in the desert. Its white walls gleamed brightly against the stark surroundings, its lone existence seeming to defy all logic.

"Hot enough for you, Pip?" Wade teased, relishing in the oppressive heat that had Piper wiping beads of sweat from her forehead. She shot him a half-hearted glare before turning her attention back to the store.

"Something feels off," she murmured, her gaze darting around the empty expanse beyond the store where the sun blazed relentlessly over the desolate Arizona landscape, casting long shadows from the cacti that dotted the red sands. "I don't like it."

"Let's not jump to conclusions," Wade said, his tone sobering as he placed a reassuring hand on her shoulder. "Keep an open mind, okay?"

Piper nodded. Inwardly, however, she couldn't shake that feeling of unease.

As they entered the store, a cool blast of air conditioning washed over them. The interior was spotless, eerily so, and the rows of neatly organized shelves seemed to mock Piper's growing discomfort. A few regulars glanced their way, their worn faces etched with curiosity and suspicion.

"Stay alert," Piper whispered to Wade, meeting the gaze of an older man who quickly looked away. Every fiber of her being screamed that there was more to this store than met the eye, and she was determined to uncover whatever secrets it held.

Her gaze zeroed in on the store owner, a slightly portly man with combed hair, a button-up shirt tucked smartly into his belt, and gleaming glasses. As they approached him, he greeted them with a smile that didn't quite reach his eyes. Wade took the lead, his protective instincts flaring as he sensed Piper's unease.

"Good afternoon, sir," Wade said, flashing his badge. "We're Agents Piper and Wade from the FBI. We'd like to ask you some questions regarding two recent customers you had." He placed a pair of photographs on the counter. "Do these women look familiar?"

The store owner's eyes flickered with recognition as he studied the pictures. "Yes, I remember them. They stopped by a few days ago. Nice girls, but nothing unusual about their visit, I'm afraid."

"Did you notice anyone suspicious in your store around that time?" Piper asked. "Anyone who might have been watching them, or who spoke to them?"

"Can't say I did," the owner replied, shaking his head. "We don't get many strangers around here. I'm sorry I can't be of more help, but I hope you find who you're looking for."

Piper's mind raced with questions, her intuition nagging at her despite the owner's seemingly genuine cooperation. She was still deciding what to say next when a middle-aged man with balding horseshoe hair emerged from the back of the store, carrying a clipboard and frowning. He looked up as he approached the owner, and there was a hitch in his step as he laid eyes on Piper and Wade.

"Uh, excuse me," he said, glancing between the agents and the owner. "I just need to ask about the items we're unpacking from the truck out back."

"Go ahead, Jim," the owner replied, his attention briefly shifting from Piper and Wade.

"No, that's alright," Jim said, flashing a greasy smile. "It can wait. I can see you're busy."

The owner shrugged, and Jim turned away, casting Piper a last fleeting glance as he disappeared through the back door. There was something troubling in that glance—not just nervousness, but genuine fear.

Fear, and maybe even anger, as well.

Piper's gaze followed Jim as he retreated through the back door, her gut churning with suspicion. She couldn't shake the feeling that something was off about him. Turning to the owner, she cleared her throat.

"Would you mind if I use your restroom?" she asked, her voice steady despite the nagging doubt tugging at her mind.

"Of course," he replied, gesturing toward a hallway. "It's just down there, second door on the right."

"Thanks," Piper said, offering a tight-lipped smile before heading in the direction indicated. But instead of turning right into the restroom, she veered left, slipping silently through the back door.

Outside, the Arizona sun scorched the ground beneath her feet as she spotted Jim unloading boxes from a truck. Sweat beaded along his forehead, his hands trembling ever so slightly. Piper approached him, her steps measured and deliberate.

"Hey," she called out, making him jump. "Are you here a lot?"

"Uh, yeah," he said, wiping his brow with the back of his hand. "Is there something I can help you with?"

"Were you working here three days ago?"

This time, there was a long, calculating pause. "Maybe," Jim said slowly. "I'd have to check."

"There was a woman here, Laurel Higgins." She pulled a photograph from her pocket and held it out. "Do you recognize her?"

The man stared at the photograph, his jaw working back and forth. He shifted the box in his hands as if uncomfortable with the weight.

Then, with a suddenness that surprised Piper, Jim threw the box at her and ran.

CHAPTER EIGHT

He inhaled deeply from his hand-rolled cigarette, savoring the acrid smoke as it curled into his lungs. His calloused fingers tightened around the worn steering wheel of his truck as a familiar tingle spread through his body.

The voices were speaking again. He did not need the drug, a desert herb colloquially known as "dream fever," in order to hear the voices, but it certainly helped to clear his mind and open him to their influence.

They were influencing him now, guiding his gaze to the dusty Jeep ahead, where he could see a young woman sitting behind the wheel, oblivious to the destiny that awaited her as she bustled along the highway.

She has no idea what's about to happen to her, he thought, a smile creeping across his weathered face. *She thinks she's safe, but she's not. No one is safe from what's coming.*

He took one last drag from his cigarette before flicking it out the window and accelerating his truck, the tires kicking up a cloud of dirt as he pursued the unsuspecting woman. He could hear the voices urging him on, whispering their plans for her fate.

As he drew closer, he could see her blonde hair whipping in the wind through the open windows of her Jeep. She was singing along to a song on the radio, completely unaware of the danger that lurked behind her.

Just like the ones who came before her. Lost in their own worlds, completely oblivious, as if I was just...invisible.

He clenched the steering wheel harder as he thought of all the women throughout his life who had overlooked him, who had never seen him for the powerful force he truly was. But that was all about to change with this woman. She was going to see him, to recognize the greatness within him.

She wouldn't have any other choice.

He took another hit of dream fever and drifted into memories of soft flesh yielding under his hands, the metallic scent of blood, and the euphoria of watching souls escape ruined bodies.

The vision of dead eyes, vacant and staring up at him in horror, filled his mind. Killing gave him a sense of power that he had never experienced in any other way. It was his purpose, his reason for being alive.

And soon, the woman in the Jeep would understand that, too.

The Jeep slowed and turned onto a narrow dirt road, heading toward a remote trailhead. The man's pulse quickened in anticipation. The spirit had led him to another sinner in need of judgment.

He stubbed out the smoldering blunt in a makeshift ashtray and accelerated, a familiar hunger awakening inside him. The hunt was on.

Tonight, he would again become immortal.

The man eased off the gas as he approached the trailhead, watching the young woman emerge from her Jeep. She stretched her arms overhead, revealing a trim midriff between her tank top and hiking shorts.

His gaze lingered on her exposed skin as she slathered on sunscreen, already picturing the constellation of bruises that would soon blossom across her flesh.

When she set off down the trail, he waited a few minutes before killing the engine on his truck. The sun beat down in a brassy sky while cicadas buzzed in the surrounding brush. Some small animal skittered through the undergrowth, fleeing as the door of his truck creaked open.

The man retrieved a backpack and a few essential supplies from behind the seat. At the bottom of the bag, his calloused fingers closed around a familiar handle.

He preferred to use his hands, but the knife was a useful tool when the spirit demanded a swifter sacrifice.

Slinging the backpack over one shoulder, he set off down the trail at an easy lope. The young woman had a decent head start, but he was in no hurry. The hunt was as much a part of the thrill as the kill.

Besides, he knew these trails well. He would chase her until exhaustion slowed her pace, and fear rattled her senses. Only then would he emerge from the shadows, watching her realization dawn that she was already dead.

A smile curled his chapped lips as he moved deeper into the wilderness. Here, he was in his element. The woman ahead was merely a fly that had wandered into his web.

He quickened his stride, guided by her scent and the whispers of the spirit in his mind. Her screams would be music to his ears, a prelude to the sublime chorus of her final breaths.

he might be invisible to her now...but that would soon change. He would, in fact, be the last thing she ever saw.

CHAPTER NINE

Piper's heart raced as she sprinted after Jim, her legs pumping furiously to keep pace. The box he had thrown at her lay crushed on the ground behind her; its contents spilled out like a gutted fish.

"Jim! Stop!" she shouted, but he only quickened his pace, darting around the corner of Friendly Fred's and disappearing into the junkyard behind it. Piper cursed under her breath, her eyes scanning the twisted, rusty maze that stretched before her.

Where'd he go? she wondered.

Seeing no sense in hesitating, she plunged headlong into the labyrinth, her brain on high alert as she attempted to anticipate Jim's next move. The sun beat down mercilessly overhead, casting stark shadows that seemed to shift and dance as she ran. Sweat poured down her face, stinging her eyes, but she blinked it away and pressed on.

Where are you, Wade she wondered? She hoped that her partner would catch up soon. He must have seen her go through the back door, and must have realized she was following Jim. She hoped he wasn't still back in the store, talking to the owner.

The junkyard seemed to go on forever, an endless graveyard of rusted metal and shattered glass. Every step she took threatened to betray her with some hidden danger—a jagged edge waiting to slice open her ankle, a buried tire ready to trip her up.

He has to be here somewhere, she thought, her eyes darting back and forth as she searched for any sign of her quarry. Jim had to be close—she could practically feel him breathing down her neck as he played cat and mouse with her in this strange maze.

Then, suddenly, she saw a flash of movement in the corner of her eye, briefly glimpsing Jim's tattered shirt as he darted behind a stack of crushed cars. Piper's pulse quickened as she zeroed in on her target, her muscles tensing like coiled springs.

Got you now, she thought, gritting her teeth as she rounded the corner, ready to confront him at last.

To her surprise, however, she discovered only a dead end. The towering stacks of rusted scrap swallowed up any trace of Jim's movements. She cursed under her breath, her heart racing in her chest as she turned in a circle.

"Think, think," she muttered, scanning the area for any signs of his passage. "Where would he go?"

Then she noticed a small gap in an adjoining fence. That must have been where Jim squeezed through. She was about to follow when it occurred to her that this was what Jim wanted—for her to keep chasing him, wandering deeper and deeper into this maze she knew nothing about.

I'm done playing games.

Climbing up the stack of crushed cars, she gazed across the junkyard. There he was, not far away, running through a row of appliances that curved steadily to the right.

Rather than chasing after Jim, Piper trotted along the top of the fence, careful not to lose her balance, and positioned herself just ahead of where Jim was going. She crouched down, waiting.

As Jim appeared, rushing around a bend in the junkyard, Piper lunged. Her body collided with his, sending them both crashing to the ground amidst a shower of dust and debris. They grappled, limbs entangled, as each fought for control.

"Get off me!" Jim shouted, his voice raw with panic.

"Stop fighting!" Piper said, pinning him to the ground. "You brought this on yourself!"

Piper's heart pounded in her chest, a mix of adrenaline and lingering anger as she held Jim down. Her breaths came in short, uneven gasps, and she could feel the grit of the junkyard beneath her knees.

"What the hell is going on?" Wade said as he caught up, his voice strained from running. He was panting heavily, sweat beading on his forehead and darkening his shirt around the collar.

"Jim here decided to throw a box at me and run," Piper replied tersely, her grip still firm on Jim's arms. "Not the smartest play."

"Sounds like he's got some explaining to do," Wade said.

"I'm not saying anything," Jim snarled, yanking his arm from Piper's grasp. He scooted away, pressing his back to a stack of cracked tires. "You ain't got nothing on me."

"Really?" Piper said. "I don't know if you're aware, but throwing a box at a federal agent is considered assault. I wouldn't call that nothing."

"Not to mention it makes him look good for the murders," Wade added. "But you wouldn't know anything about that, would you?"

Jim lowered his eyes, looking sullen."Of course I know about the murders. Everyone in town's talking about them. Doesn't mean I was involved, though."

"You sure have a funny way of proving your innocence," Piper said.

Jim glared at her, his jaw clenched. Finally, he shook his head bitterly and looked away as if there was no point trying to explain anything to her.

"Jim, we're just trying to find the truth," Wade said, attempting to reason with him. "We're not here to hurt you or anyone else. If you've got information that can help us—"

"Information?" Jim interrupted, his eyes darting between Piper and Wade. "What kind of information do you want? How about the fact that I'm terrified every single day? That I can't sleep at night because I'm too damn scared?"

"Scared of what, though?" Piper asked, puzzled by this turn.

"Of being caught!" Jim exploded, tears streaming down his face, mixing with the dirt and sweat that coated his skin. "You think this is easy for me? You think I just decided one day to be a part of this whole mess?"

Piper could hardly believe her ears. Was he really about to confess to everything? Could it be so simple?

"Jim," she said, "it sounds like you need to get something off your chest. So whatever you know about these murders—"

"I didn't murder anyone!"

Piper frowned, puzzled. "No? Then what are you talking about?"

Jim looked away, clamping his mouth shut.

"You're in too far to turn back now, partner," Wade said. "Unless you want to face a charge for assaulting a federal officer…"

Jim sighed, and with that sigh, all the fight seemed to go out of him, as if he finally realized how trapped he was. He swallowed hard, his eyes darting between Piper and Wade before settling on a spot somewhere in the distance.

"There's this… herb," he began, his voice cracking slightly. "It grows out in the desert—rare stuff. Some people say it's got healing properties, but that ain't all. It's also a powerful hallucinogen. People around here have been using it for years."

"Go on," Piper said, her pulse quickening at the thought of a potential lead.

"Thing is, not everyone can handle it," Jim continued, fiddling with a frayed thread poking out from the cuff of his shirt. "Some folks lose their minds—see things that ain't there. Makes 'em do things they wouldn't normally do."

He paused, frowning as if trying to remember his point. "Anyway," he said, "that's why I ran. I saw the pictures, and..." He trailed off, coloring a little.

It took Piper a moment to connect the dots. "You sold it to one of the victims," she said.

He nodded. "Laurel, I think her name was. Heard about her murder, so then when you two showed up, waving her picture around, I figured you were going to try to pin the murder on me."

It made sense. Piper was not ready to believe his innocence quite yet, however. She needed a bit more proof.

"Jim," she said, "where were you last night?"

Jim ran a hand through his unkempt hair. Then he grunted, shaking his head and smiling ruefully.

"What?" Piper asked.

"It's just funny, is all."

"What is?"

"I was at my son's basketball game. Only one I've been to all year. Tough getting away, you know?"

"And the night before?" Piper asked, her disappointment growing as she sensed that Jim might indeed be innocent.

"Down in El Paso, watching a rodeo with some friends. I can give you their names, if you want."

"That'd be great," Wade said.

Piper stopped listening as Jim shared this information with Wade. She felt detached from herself as if watching from a distance. Numb. She'd hoped they might have caught a break in the case, but now it appeared they were back to square one.

The only difference was that the sun had slipped a little closer to the horizon. Before long, it would be dark.

And the killer would be free to strike again.

CHAPTER TEN

Piper's heart was as heavy as a stone in her chest as she stared at the facade of the rundown motel. A flickering neon sign cast an eerie glow on the gravel parking lot, illuminating patches of weeds that fought for dominance between the cracks.

"It kills you, doesn't it?" Wade asked quietly. "Having to take a break."

"Knowing the killer is still out there?" She pressed her lips together bitterly and nodded. "Yes, it does. He could be stalking his next victim as we speak."

"That's true. But we won't do anyone any good if we're falling down from exhaustion."

As much as Piper hated to admit it, she knew Wade was right. They needed rest. She just hoped the killer needed it as much as they did.

With a heavy sigh, Piper got out of the SUV. The desert air was heavy with the scent of dust and gasoline fumes, mingling with the faint aroma of stale cigarettes that seemed to swim around them. The sound of traffic hurrying by on the nearby highway filled the air, a constant reminder of the world passing them by as they were forced to pause in their pursuit of justice.

The motel was a relic from a time long past, its crumbling facade standing as a testament to the slow decay of the surrounding area. Paint peeled away from the walls like old skin, revealing the weathered wood beneath. The windows were filmy with grime, making it hard to discern whether there was any life stirring within.

Piper couldn't help but feel a swell of disappointment at the sight. She had been driven to succeed in her career, fueled by the memories of both her past failures and successes. This case was no different; she was relentless in her pursuit, determined to bring the killer to justice. And yet, here she was, stuck in a place that seemed to embody everything she was fighting against.

"Don't worry," Wade said, his voice cutting through Piper's thoughts like a knife. "We'll be back on the case first thing in the morning."

Piper nodded, knowing he was right.

As they entered the dingy motel lobby, the atmosphere of discouragement and poverty enveloped them like a shroud. The smell of stale cigarette smoke and cheap cleaning products assaulted Piper's nostrils. The wallpaper was peeling and faded, as though even it wanted to escape the dreary confines of the motel. An air of despair clung to the place, as tangible as the dust that danced in the sparse beams of light from the flickering fluorescent bulbs overhead.

"Feels like the kind of place where dreams come to die," Piper muttered under her breath.

"Can I help you?" The voice belonged to a portly man with thin gray hair combed over his scalp in a futile attempt to hide his baldness. He stood behind the reception desk, eyeing them with an expression that suggested they were just another inconvenience in his day.

"Uh, yeah," Wade said, adjusting his grip on his duffle bag. "We need a room for the night."

"Only got one left," the clerk replied, not bothering to look up from his crossword puzzle. "Most of the place is under renovation." He gestured vaguely toward an area sectioned off by yellow caution tape.

Looks like the whole place could use some renovation, Piper thought, but she kept this to herself. Instead, she exchanged a glance with Wade, who simply shrugged in response.

"Guess we'll take it," she said, trying to keep the disappointment out of her voice.

"Keys are on the counter," the clerk said, returning his attention to his puzzle as if they had ceased to exist.

"Thanks," Wade said, grabbing the key.

As they walked down the dimly lit hallway, Piper felt a knot forming in her stomach. She and Wade had been partners for a number of years before her year-long hiatus in Alaska, and they'd had to share a room on more than one occasion, but she felt her cheeks growing warm at the thought nonetheless. The sensation was both thrilling and nerve-wracking.

"Home sweet home," Wade muttered as he pushed open the door. The hinges creaked as if protesting their intrusion, and the dim, musty room that greeted them didn't exactly help to dispel Piper's unease.

"Looks like it's seen better days," she said, trying to keep her tone light as she surveyed the cracked paint on the walls and the threadbare carpet beneath their feet.

"Better than sleeping in the car, though, right?" Wade said with a grin. "Besides, I've slept in worse places. Nothing as bad as the frigid Arctic, though, I'm sure."

As they continued to take in their surroundings, Piper couldn't quite shake the feeling of awkwardness that had settled between them. Her gaze was drawn toward the single bed against the far wall.

"I'm used to sleeping outside, you know," she said, attempting to sound nonchalant. "I don't mind taking the floor."

Wade shook his head. "No way, Pip. It wouldn't be right for me to let you sleep on the floor while I take the bed. Besides, there aren't even any extra blankets or pillows."

She was about to suggest they flip a coin to decide who got the bed when a cockroach darted across the floor, disappearing under the dresser. Piper suppressed a shudder.

"Looks like we've got company," she said with a grimace.

"Guess that makes the decision easier," Wade said. "We'll both sleep in the bed."

Piper's heart gave a sharp beat, both excited and nervous. She avoided Wade's eyes, unsure what to say.

"I'll sleep the opposite way," Wade continued, "with my head by your feet."

"Alright," Piper agreed, trying to ignore the butterflies fluttering in her stomach.

They both began their nighttime routines, avoiding each other's gaze as they brushed their teeth and changed into their sleepwear. The tension in the room was palpable, and Piper could feel her heart hammering in her chest. Even though they had worked plenty of cases together and had dealt with plenty of unusual sleeping arrangements, this time felt different. Maybe it was the fact that they'd gone a year without seeing one another, long enough for Piper to realize there was something special between her and Wade, something more than just professional respect.

As they finally settled into the bed, the awkwardness only increased. They lay there, heads at opposite ends of the bed, limbs stiff as though afraid to make contact. The silence was deafening, punctuated only by the hum of the air conditioner and the occasional distant rush of traffic on the highway.

"Goodnight, Pip," Wade said quietly, his voice tinged with amusement.

"Goodnight, Wade." She tried not to think about how close he was, even if their positions were reversed. Was he as nervous as she was? Did he sense her presence as she sensed his?

In the darkness, her mind wandered back to their case. She thought about her past failures and the endless drive that pushed her forward, making her relentless in her pursuit of justice.

And now, here she was, sharing a bed with her partner. As strange as it was, she was glad to have Wade nearby. He had always been there to support her, to help level her out when she felt like she was spiraling. He understood her need for success, even when it threatened to consume her.

Despite the unusual circumstances, Piper felt a strange sense of comfort knowing he was there, just inches away. It was a testament to the trust they'd built over time, a trust that would surely only grow stronger as they continued to work together.

"Sweet dreams, Pip," Wade murmured, his voice barely audible above the hum of the air conditioner.

"Same to you," she whispered back, closing her eyes.

And before she knew it, she was asleep.

She dreamed she was standing before her childhood home, its once vibrant paint now chipped and faded. The front door hung crookedly on its hinges, creaking softly in the breeze. She glanced around, trying to place herself within the timeline of her life, but nothing seemed to fit. It was as if she had been transported to a time that didn't exist, a limbo between reality and memory.

As she approached the house, her heart pounded in her chest. Her hands shook with a mixture of fear and anticipation, and she couldn't help but wonder what awaited her inside. This was a moment she had relived countless times, both waking and sleeping.

The day her mother went missing.

Despite the dread clawing at her insides, Piper forced herself to step through the doorway. The house was eerily silent, the air thick with tension. She could sense that something was wrong, but her dream-self couldn't quite grasp the significance of these events. All she knew was that she had to find her mother.

"Mom?" she called, her voice small and uncertain. There was no response, only the distant echo of her own words bouncing back at her.

Her feet moved of their own accord, propelling her through the familiar rooms of her childhood. The house seemed to have been frozen in time, every detail exactly as she remembered it. She could almost believe her mother would appear at any moment, laughing and scolding her for worrying.

And yet, Piper knew deep down that wouldn't happen. The weight of the truth bore down on her like a crushing force, suffocating her until she could hardly breathe. Her mother was gone, and she had never found any answers.

The dream continued to unravel around her, plunging her deeper into the past even as it threatened to consume her entirely.

"Mom? Where are you?" Piper's voice quivered with emotion, but there was no answer, only the oppressive silence that had haunted her ever since that fateful day.

CHAPTER ELEVEN

The harsh fluorescent light of the rest stop bathroom cast a sickly pallor on Karla's face as she leaned over the sink, splashing cold water on her cheeks. As the water ran down, she traced the lines etched around her eyes and mouth, a cruel reminder of the passing years.

You're not a spring chicken anymore, she thought.

Faced with this reminder of her own mortality, she couldn't help but think of her mother, whose own face had been marred by wrinkles borne from a lifetime of bitterness and disappointment. It was an unsettling comparison, given their strained relationship.

"God, I look like her," she muttered under her breath, the words resonating off the grimy tiles. She straightened up, gripping the edge of the porcelain sink, and stared at her reflection in the smudged mirror. The funeral loomed ahead like a dark cloud, and she wished nothing more than to have it over with and be on her way.

That was why she'd resolved to drive through the night, ignoring her exhaustion. She just wanted to be done with it—with the funeral, with all the arrangements and sympathy cards, and most of all, with her mother. It was a cruel thing to think, yes, but she meant it no less.

The truth was, her mother had been dead to her for a long time.

As the water dripped from her chin, Karla found her gaze drawn to the slow whirlpool forming in the clogged drain. Watching the water's languid descent, memories of her childhood bubbled to the surface. She remembered the countless nights of her mother's alcohol-fueled rages, punctuated by the slamming of doors as yet another boyfriend stormed out. She recalled how her mother would pass out on the couch, glassy-eyed and reeking of cheap whiskey, leaving Karla to fend for herself.

"Eighteen," she whispered, her voice thick with emotion. That was the magic number, the age at which she had finally left her mother's squalid apartment and never looked back. She shook her head, trying to dispel the ghosts of the past, and reached for a paper towel to dry her face.

"You need to keep moving," she told herself firmly, her eyes meeting her reflection. "You've been stuck in the past too long already. Go bury your mother…and then move on with your life."

With renewed purpose, Karla stepped out of the bathroom and into the dimly lit rest stop. The vending machine hummed in the corner, its garish lights beckoning her with the promise of caffeine—just what she needed to help finish her drive.

As she scanned the rows of brightly colored energy drinks, however, she realized she didn't have any change. Not so much as a single penny.

"Damn it," she muttered, casting a glance toward her parked car outside. The night was dark and quiet, a stark contrast to the constant roar of the highway behind her. She hesitated for a moment before pushing open the door, the hinges squeaking in protest.

The air outside was cool and damp, heavy with the scent of decay as insects rustled and chirred in the underbrush just beyond the reach of the rest stop's feeble lights. Karla shivered, feeling vulnerable and exposed as she hurried to her car, hoping to find some loose change inside.

She fumbled with the keys, finally unlocking the door and yanking it open. She checked the console, the glove box, and even between the seats, her fingers brushing against lint and old receipts. Just when she was about to give up, a glint caught her eye—a quarter wedged firmly between the driver's seat and the console. Where there was one, there were bound to be more.

"Gotcha," she murmured, bending down to retrieve it. Her arm strained as she forced it between the unforgiving plastic and yielding fabric, fingertips grazing the cold metal of the coin. With a triumphant grunt, she managed to pry it loose, holding it up to the light in victory.

"Finally," she sighed, turning to head back to the vending machine.

And that was when she saw the man standing beside her, his face half-hidden in shadow. A flicker of recognition passed through her mind, but she couldn't quite place him.

"Who—" she began, but that was all she managed before his hands shot out, wrapping themselves around her throat and choking out the words. She struggled, scratching at his hands and kicking at his legs, but nothing relieved the pressure.

Darkness swam in her vision, growing and growing until it swallowed her whole.

CHAPTER TWELVE

Piper's sleep was fitful, a collage of fragmented images and feelings. She found herself in the body of her teenage self, wandering a mountain trail in Alaska, her breath visible as puffs of white vapor.

"Mom?" she called, her voice trembling against the crisp air. The sunlit mountain peaks glistened like some sort of postcard paradise, but Piper felt the weight of nameless dread pressing down on her.

"Mom!" she cried again, her voice cracking with urgency. Her eyes fixed on the dark forest ahead, a stark contrast to the surrounding cheeriness. It was as though night had seeped into the trees and refused to leave, casting shadows that swallowed all light.

Piper hesitated. Her heart pounded in her chest before she took one step after another toward the darkness. Something compelled her to move forward, drawn by a magnetic force toward the unknown.

Her gaze dropped to the muddy path, and there they were—her mother's footprints. Her heart skipped a beat as she noticed the irregularity in the tracks, the telltale signs of a limp. Her mind raced with concern for her mother's safety as a sickening feeling settled in her gut. She couldn't shake the premonition that something terrible had happened.

"Mom, where are you?" Her voice wavered as it echoed through the sinister forest. Each step she took was heavier than the last, weighed down by the unspoken terror that awaited her just beyond the treeline.

Piper's pulse quickened as she entered the foreboding woods. Everything about the place screamed danger, and yet she couldn't turn back. She had to find her mother. With each hesitant step, Piper delved deeper into the darkness, following the injured tracks of the woman who had given her life. The cold gnawed at her bones, but she pushed forward, driven by an instinctive need to protect and save.

"Please, Mom..." Piper whispered, her breath hitching. "Please be okay."

This alien forest was nothing like the sunlit mountains she had left behind. Here, only darkness reigned. She reached out, her fingers brushing against the rough bark of a tree, seeking reassurance that this nightmare was real.

"Please, Mom, answer me," she pleaded, her voice cracking with desperation. But the forest remained silent, indifferent to her plight. Panic bubbled inside her, threatening to consume her. With each step, the feeling of dread intensified, suffocating her like a shroud.

Her thoughts raced as her mind grappled for an explanation. What could have happened to her mother? Why was she limping through this sinister wilderness? Piper tried to focus on the footprints, but the shadows played tricks on her eyes, making them dance and blur.

"Keep going, Piper," she told herself, forcing her legs to move. "You can't give up now." She willed herself to stay strong, to push past the terror that clawed at her insides.

As she ventured deeper into the forest, the darkness seemed to grow thicker, pressing in on her from all sides. The faint rustlings grew louder, like whispers in the night, urging her to turn back. But Piper knew she couldn't. She had to find her mother, no matter what horrors lay ahead.

"Mom!" she shouted, pouring every ounce of determination into her voice. "I'm coming for you!"

Through the oppressive gloom, a shape began to emerge, its form twisted and unnatural. Piper squinted at the dark silhouette, her heart pounding in her chest. As she drew closer, the shadows receded, revealing an old building swallowed by the forest. Vines slithered across its surface like serpents, their movements sinister and unsettling.

"Byron Gray's house," Piper whispered, her voice barely audible over the rustling of the leaves. She remembered when the man had masqueraded as Professor Benjamin Graham, a deceit that had nearly cost her everything. The thought sent a shiver down her spine, and her dread deepened.

Mom must be in there, she thought.

Gathering her courage, Piper reached for the door handle. The cold metal bit into her trembling fingers. She took a deep breath, steadied herself, and swung the door open. A gust of stale air escaped from within, carrying with it the scent of decay and forgotten memories.

As she stepped inside, the darkness enveloped her, swallowing her whole. "Mom, where are you?" she cried; her voice echoed through the empty halls. The house remained silent, offering no solace or answers.

Her heart raced as she ventured deeper into the house, each step weighed down by dread. The walls seemed to close in on her, the shadows shifting and dancing like specters. But it wasn't until she rounded a corner that she realized the horrifying truth: she hadn't entered a house at all.

Instead, she stood within the gaping maw of some monstrous creature, its teeth gnashing hungrily around her. Panic surged through her, a primal fear threatening to drown her reason.

"Let me go!" Piper screamed, her voice high and shrill. She clawed at the walls, desperate to escape the creature's grasp. But with each frantic movement, the mouth closed tighter, sealing her in darkness.

"Please!" she sobbed, her tears mingling with the cold saliva that dripped from the creature's gums. "I just want to find my mom!"

As the jaws tightened around her, Piper's world began to fade, consumed by an all-encompassing blackness. The last thing she heard was the sound of her own heart pounding in her ears, a futile cry for help swallowed by the void.

* * *

Piper jolted awake, gasping for air as the remnants of her nightmare clung to her like a cold sweat. The bedside lamp cast a warm glow over the motel room, but it did little to chase away the shadows that still seemed to press in around her. The clock on the nightstand read 3:43, and Wade was shaking her awake, his large hands gripping her shoulders with a firm gentleness.

"Mom..." she mumbled, her voice thick with sleep and fear. She sat up, disoriented, and wiped her eyes. "I... I had a dream about her. I was looking for her, and as I went through the forest I came across this house…"

She paused, noticing for the first time that Wade was fully dressed. There was something in his eyes, too—a weariness that spoke of more than physical fatigue.

"What's going on?" she asked, propping herself up on an elbow. "What happened?"

"Another murder," Wade replied grimly. "It seems our killer's not wasting any time."

* * *

The rest stop was deserted when they arrived, save for a few semis parked haphazardly in the designated spots. The harsh glare of the overhead lights cast long shadows across the pavement, and the smell of diesel hung heavy in the air. Piper shivered as she stepped out of the car, her breath visible in the chilly night air.

"Damn, it's cold," Wade muttered, stuffing his hands into the pockets of his coat. He glanced over at Piper, who was lost in thought. "You still thinking about that dream?"

Piper tore her gaze from the empty expanse of the parking lot and nodded. "It felt so real," she admitted, her voice barely above a whisper. "Something about it just… it's hard to shake."

"Sometimes dreams can be like that," Wade said, his tone gentle. "But it's just a dream, Pip. I need you in the here and now, okay?"

She nodded again, forcing herself to push the nightmare aside in favor of the task at hand. "Where was the body found?"

"Over there, I think," he said, nodding to a spot near the edge of the parking lot. A lone vehicle sat in the shadows, separated from the rows of trucks. A tarp covered a still form beside it, the sight making Piper's stomach churn.

"I hope this is the last one," she whispered, her breath coming out in small puffs of vapor. Wade's large hand gently squeezed her shoulder, a wordless gesture of reassurance.

Piper crouched down next to the tarp, and Wade slowly pulled it back.

The victim was a woman, her face contorted in a silent scream. Her eyes bulged, bloodshot and wide open, as if pleading for help that would never come. Her skin was tinged a sickly shade of blue, the result of suffocation. Piper felt a surge of anger and sadness as she studied the woman's features.

"Another innocent life taken," she murmured, her voice full of sorrow. Wade nodded solemnly, his jaw clenched in frustration.

"Let's see if we can find any identification." Piper reached into the victim's pocket and retrieved a wallet. She flipped it open, revealing the driver's license. "Her name was Karla. She's from Tennessee."

"Long way from home," Wade said.

Piper lowered the wallet and looked around, thinking about the location of the rest stop in relation to the sites where the previous two victims were found.

"We must be, what, thirty or forty miles from the place Laurel's body was discovered?" she asked.

Wade considered for a moment, then nodded. "Sounds about right."

"The killer doesn't have any problem moving around," Piper muttered. "He might attack from the desert, but that doesn't mean he doesn't use the roads, too."

"Which means he could be anywhere."

Piper nodded, her heart heavy with the realization that they still had no solid leads to follow. The killer was elusive, always one step ahead of them, and it left her feeling powerless.

"Whoever's doing this, he's not going to stop on his own," she whispered. She looked at Wade, his dark eyes reflecting the same resolve that burned within her.

"We won't let him," Wade said, his voice low and determined. "We'll find him. And we'll make him pay."

Piper nodded, feeling a sense of solidarity with her partner. They couldn't let the killer continue to take innocent lives. They needed to stop him before he struck again.

But as she stood there in the cool night air, staring at the lifeless body of another victim, the memory of her nightmare crept back into her mind: those monstrous jaws opened wide, swallowing her whole, swallowing her screams.

CHAPTER THIRTEEN

"Three victims now," Piper began thoughtfully. "All strangled. All killed without leaving any witnesses."

They were standing a short distance from the food truck where they had each just purchased a burrito. Despite how wonderful the food smelled, Piper's stomach twisted at the thought of eating so soon after the discovery of the last victim's body. She stared down at the meal in her hands, her appetite waning as the grisly images from the crime scene threatened to overwhelm her. She gripped the burrito hard enough to cause the filling to start oozing out the end, her jaw set in a tight line.

The morning sun blazed overhead, casting a golden glow on the desert landscape as she and Wade stood in line at the food truck. The air shimmered with heat, and the scent of sizzling meat and spices wafted in the gentle breeze. Sweat dampened Piper's brow, but it wasn't just from the rising temperatures. The memory of the third victim's contorted face still haunted her, the lifeless eyes staring into nothingness.

Wade swallowed a mouthful of burrito and gazed at her with concern. "You gotta eat, Pip."

Piper swallowed hard, trying to force the bile back down her throat as she relaxed her hands. "Sorry, it's just… after seeing that poor girl's body..."

Wade nodded sympathetically. "I know how you feel, but we need to keep our strength up. We can't let this bastard win by breaking us down."

"Easy for you to say," Piper muttered, her gaze drifting over to the food truck driver, who seemed blissfully unaware of the horrors they'd witnessed that morning.

"Look," Wade said, leaning in closer. "We're the only ones who can stop this killer, and we can't do that on an empty stomach. It doesn't have to be a lot, but just try to eat something, okay?"

Piper sighed, her shoulders sagging under the weight of his words. He was right. They needed to remain focused and energized if they were going to bring justice to the victims and their families.

Steeling herself, she took a bite of the burrito and forced herself to chew, the movements mechanical.

"There you go," Wade said. He frowned and armed sweat from his forehead with his arm. "No signs the victims managed to fight back," he added, following up on the remark Piper had made earlier. "Our killer's efficient—brutally so."

"Almost surgical. Whoever he is, he knows what he's doing."

"Experienced?" Wade asked, his dark eyes meeting hers.

"Definitely," she confirmed, swallowing hard as she thought back to the gruesome crime scenes. "But there's more to it than that. All the victims were found within a fifty-mile radius of each other, right here in the desert. It's like he's marking his territory."

"Like a predator," Wade said, his brow furrowing as he mulled over her words.

"Exactly. And predators don't just spring up overnight, do they? They hone their skills, learn the lay of the land. I think our guy has been at this for a long time."

"Longer than we thought, you mean?" Wade asked as he finished the last of his burrito.

"Much longer," Piper replied, her fingers tapping thoughtfully on the foil within which her own half-eaten breakfast was wrapped. "I'd be willing to bet there are more bodies out there—ones we haven't connected to him yet."

"Unsolved cases, you think?" Wade asked, his eyes narrowing in thought.

"Could be." Piper took a deep breath as she steeled herself for the task ahead. "We need to go through the local records, see if there are any other crimes that match our killer's MO. It's a long shot, but it could help us pinpoint just how long he's been active." She paused, turning over the implications in her mind.

"And maybe," she continued, "give us a clue about where he'll strike next."

* * *

A sense of foreboding descended on Piper like a shadow as they entered the police station. A hum of activity washed over them, the familiar cacophony of ringing phones, clattering keyboards, and hushed conversations providing a sense of order amidst the chaos of their investigation.How many more bodies, Piper wondered, might they link to their killer? How many deaths might he be responsible for?

They navigated through the maze of desks and filing cabinets, the sound of their footsteps muffled by the worn carpet beneath them. Eventually, they reached a dimly lit corner of the station, where rows of metal shelves loomed over them like silent sentinels guarding long-forgotten secrets.

"Here we are," said Piper, her voice hushed in reverence of the somber atmosphere. "Cold cases. Where hope comes to die."

"Or where it gets resurrected," countered Wade, his brow furrowed in concentration as his eyes scanned the labels on the spines of the dusty case files. "If there's any connection between our guy and these other murders, it'll be in here somewhere."

"Let's hope so," muttered Piper, reaching for one of the folders at random. She pulled it from the shelf, the once crisp paper now softened and yellowed with age, and began flipping through the pages.

"So we're looking for any unsolved murders in the area," Piper said, "preferably with similar MOs to our guy."

"Right," Wade said. "I'll start with anything from the past five years. You go further back—maybe ten or fifteen?"

Piper pulled open a drawer filled with dusty, long-forgotten files. "Sounds good."

As they began poring over the cold cases, the rustling of papers filled the air. The second rolled by like hours as they meticulously searched for patterns, connections, and clues that might link their killer to other crimes.

Slowly but surely, a chilling picture began to emerge. Cases dating back decades bore striking similarities to their current investigation—the same brutal methods, the same eerie precision, and the same absence of any discernible motive. It was becoming increasingly clear that they were dealing with a predator who had been stalking his prey for years, honing his skills and evading capture at every turn.

"Look at this," Piper said, her voice strained as she held up a file from fifteen years prior. "This victim was strangled in the exact same way as our victims. And there are more—all unsolved, all eerily similar."

Wade shook his head; frustration was etched on his face. "But we can't prove it's him, Pip," he said, his voice heavy with disappointment. "He could have picked up on the methods used by other killers or even taught them to others."

"Maybe," Piper said. "But something about this feels different, Wade. Like we're dealing with a single, relentless force—one that's been hiding in plain sight for far too long."

As they sat back in their chairs, Piper was struck by the enormity of their task. She sensed they were getting closer to unmasking this monster, but without concrete evidence, they were powerless to bring him to justice.

She sighed. Her eyes were clouded with questions. What drove this killer to commit such heinous acts? And how had he managed to evade capture for so long?

It's like the desert is his accomplice, she thought, pausing for a moment to rub her tired eyes. *It swallows up secrets like it swallows up life—relentlessly, without mercy.*

The stack of dusty files grew larger on the table, casting a shadow over Piper as she delved deeper into the details of each case. The stench of stale coffee and cigarette smoke hung in the air, mingling with the faint scent of ink and old paper. The distant sound of ringing phones and hurried footsteps echoed around them, but it all faded to nothing as Piper's focus narrowed to the chilling pages before her.

"Here," she said, sliding another file toward Wade. "Eight years ago. Same MO as our victims."

"Damn," muttered Wade, running a hand through his hair. "The more we find, the worse it gets." He leaned closer to study the photographs, suppressing a shudder at the sight of the pale, lifeless face staring back at him. "But we're still missing something, Pip. There's got to be a connection between the victims."

Piper chewed on her pen, eyes scanning the words on the page as if they held the key to unlocking the mystery. Her brow furrowed, deep in thought. "You're right. There has to be a reason he chose these women, but what?" She sighed, her frustration palpable.

She picked up another file and began reading. The victim, twenty-five-year-old Ella Adams, was found strangled to death in her car just off the highway. Witnesses spotted a green sedan leaving the scene of the crime.

"Look at this," she said excitedly, turning the file around so that Wade could read it. "We might just have a description of the vehicle. It's not much to go on, I know, but maybe Luke or someone else at the motel saw a similar vehicle…" She trailed off, puzzled by the expression on Wade's face as he studied the file. He looked like he was holding something back.

"What?" she asked.

"Pip…" He let out a slow sigh. "Ella was strangled with a length of telephone cable. Plus, she wasn't from out-of-state—grew up right in the area."

Piper sank back, disappointed. "How'd I miss that?" she asked. She grabbed the file so she could examine it for herself again.

"I know how you missed it. You're exhausted."

"I got plenty of sleep last night," she countered, her gaze locked onto the papers in front of her. "He's out there, Wade. And every minute we waste is another minute he could be taking someone else."

"If you keep pushing yourself," he said carefully, "you'll just make more mistakes, and so will I. I know how badly you want to catch this guy, but the best way to do that is by taking care of yourself. Even just a few minutes will do you some good."

Piper leaned back and drummed her fingers on the table. As much as she hated to admit it, she knew Wade was right. She had missed two obvious and very significant details. If she kept going without rest, what other crucial details might she overlook?

Reluctantly she pushed back her chair and stood up. She stretched her arms overhead and feel the stiffness in her shoulders and back. "Alright," she agreed, forcing a thin smile onto her lips. "Just a few minutes."

As she stepped away from the table, she couldn't help but glance back at the ghastly photographs that littered its surface. Each one told the same story—a life stolen, a family left to grieve – and the weight of it all threatened to crush her.

Focus, she admonished herself, shaking off the creeping despair. *Don't let it get to you. This is too important.*

When she returned to the table after her short break, Wade had organized the files into a neat stack. "Did you find anything new?" she asked, her voice barely concealing her eagerness.

"Nothing concrete," he admitted, his brow creasing with frustration. "Just more questions." He rubbed the back of his neck, clearly exasperated. "We know he's been doing this for years, but we still can't tie him to all these murders. It's like trying to pin down a ghost."

As they plunged back into the sea of files, Piper couldn't shake the uneasy feeling that time was running out. With every tick of the clock, the killer remained one step ahead like a specter haunting the shadows of their investigation, eluding capture at every turn.

And she and Wade might be the only people standing between the killer and his next victim.

* * *

Piper leaned back in her chair, massaging her temples as she stared at the blurred lines of text on the screen before her. The hum of fluorescent lights and the distant chatter of officers filled the air, creating a symphony of noise that only served to heighten her growing headache. She glanced over at Wade, who was also poring over a stack of case files, his brow furrowed in concentration.

"Hey, Wade," she said, breaking the silence between them. "I've been thinking about something."

Wade looked up from his files, arching an eyebrow inquisitively. "What's on your mind, Pip?"

She hesitated for a moment, collecting her thoughts. "I've noticed a pattern in the locations of these murders," she said, gesturing to a map pinned to the wall on which she had noted in red marker the locations of bodies. "All of the crime scenes are either near the desert or in remote areas. And it got me thinking: What if our killer is some sort of desert nomad?"

"A desert nomad?" Wade repeated, clearly amused. "Like

"More like someone who's been living off the grid for years, surviving in the harsh environment of the desert," she said, ignoring his attempt at levity. "It would explain how he's managed to avoid capture for so long. He knows the terrain better than anyone, and he's able to blend in with the local community when it suits him."

Wade considered her theory and then nodded. "Yeah, I can see that. But why do you think he's targeting these particular victims? What's his motive?"

"Opportunity, maybe," she said. "Or a particular place he encounters them." She shook her head. "I'm not sure."

"Maybe there's no logic to it," Wade suggested grimly. "Maybe he just enjoys killing."

"That's possible, too," Piper said. "The more important question, I think, is what caused him to escalate his killing spree recently. If he's been active for years, why has he suddenly started killing more frequently?"

"Maybe he just snapped," Wade said, scratching his chin thoughtfully. "Or he could be facing a personal crisis—girlfriend left him, boss fired him, that kind of thing."

Piper frowned, unsure what to think. As she scanned the cold cases littered across her desk, she discovered that a number of lines had been redacted, the information simply removed from the document.

"I wonder what this is about," she said, shifting one of the files toward Wade and pointing at the section in question.

He frowned. "Seems like something we should figure out. But who do we ask?"

Piper's gaze fell on a name: Ezequiel Jimenez. Apparently he'd been the lead detective on a number of these cases.

"This Detective Jimenez could be someone worth talking to," she said, tapping his name. "Might be able to explain why some information is missing."

"If he's still around," Wade said. "Could be up there in years, given the age of some of these cases. Might've passed away."

"I hope not," Piper said, her heart sinking at the thought. "Because if he did, there's no telling what secrets might have died with him."

CHAPTER FOURTEEN

Piper and Wade pulled up at the dingy bar at the edge of town, the only place they knew of where Jimenez had been known to hang out. As Piper studied the cluster of bikes gathered outside, she felt a tightness in her stomach. She knew this could very well be a recipe for disaster, walking into a place like this and waving their badges around.

Still, they had to find Jimenez. If this was the only way to find him, then so be it.

"Strange place for a detective to hang out," Wade said.

"I was thinking the same thing," Piper said.

They left the vehicle and stepped inside the gloomy bar. It felt to Piper like walking into another world, a world filled with unseen secrets and danger. The air was thick with smoke and tension, and all eyes seemed to turn on them, regarding them warily. A few patrons murmured among themselves, making no attempt to avert their stares.

At the far end of the bar, a gruff-looking man stood behind the counter, wiping down glasses. He eyed them suspiciously as they approached.

"Can I help you?" he asked.

"We're looking for Ezequiel Jimenez," Piper said. "Do you know him?"

The barman's expression hardened further if that was even possible. "Never heard of him," he said flatly. He moved away from them and started to busy himself with other chores, clearly indicating that the conversation was over.

Piper and Wade exchanged another look. Piper couldn't tell whether the barman was being honest and simply resented their presence in his bar, perhaps picking up on the fact that they were law enforcement or whether he was hiding something. She was leaning toward the latter.

Piper opened her mouth to ask him another question, but before she could say anything, the barman cut her off. "Listen," he said, "this is a respectable establishment. You either buy something, or you leave, got it?"

The scene had quickly grown from tense to hostile, and Piper felt the eyes of the other patrons on her. As she gazed around the room, however, one man – a heavyset fellow with a gray ponytail seated in the corner and cradling a mug of beer – glanced away, staring out the window as if something else had caught his attention.

"Now are you going to buy a drink or what?" the barman asked.

Piper, following her instincts, stepped away. "Wade, why don't you get us a couple club sodas? I need to go talk to someone."

Wade nodded, a slight frown creasing his forehead as he watched her move toward the back of the room.

Piper approached the man with the ponytail slowly, trying not to draw any attention. "Excuse me," she said, her voice low and steady. "I'm looking for someone, a man by the name of Ezequiel Jimenez. Do you know him?"

The man looked up at her, his expression unreadable. He didn't answer right away; instead, he took a long sip from his mug before setting it down and turning his gaze back to the window. "Can't say I do," he finally said.

Piper studied him for a moment. It was clear to her that he was lying, but she had no idea why. He gave off a cop vibe, which led her to make an educated guess.

"You don't work with him by any chance, do you?" she asked.

The man looked at her, his eyes narrowing as if to better understand how she had known such a thing. "Who are you?" he asked.

She pulled out her badge and showed it to him. "Agent Piper Woods."

The man seemed to study the badge for a long time, as if uncertain whether he could believe it was real.

"I'm Wade," Wade said as he joined them, setting a club soda in front of Piper. "Mind if we sit with you?"

The man with the ponytail shrugged, and they sat down. He swallowed hard, and Piper noticed his gaze flicked to the exterior door as if measuring his chances of making an escape.

Finally, he sighed and leaned back, thoughtfully plucking at his beard. "Whatever you think Zeke did, he didn't do it."

The words surprised Piper. "So you *do* know him," she said.

"*Did*," he corrected. "Zeke's retired now. Haven't seen or heard from him in ages."

"Why were you so secretive when I asked about him?"

The man sighed. "Zeke and I used to be partners. He put away some of the most dangerous mob bosses out there, guys who threatened not just him but his family as well. The mob put out a hit on Zeke, and he's been very secretive since. That's part of the reason he quit the force."

He paused for a moment before continuing. "You know, Zeke was the sort of guy who could get things done when no one else could. He sacrificed his own safety for justice—not many people can say that."

Piper nodded, feeling admiration for the man even though she'd never met him. "What about you?" she asked. "Aren't you worried?"

The man shrugged, smiling. "Me? I missed out on most of the excitement, I'm afraid. Chemo—skin cancer. Mob's not particularly interested in me." He chuckled darkly.

"What did you say your name was?"

"Didn't. Caleb Parch, at your service."

"Well, Caleb, we really need to find Zeke. Any idea where he could be living?"

Caleb shook his head. "Don't know and don't want to know. I owe him that much."

Piper pursed her lips, trying to think of the best way to convince Caleb of the seriousness of the situation. "We're investigating a series of murders that might be linked to cold cases Zeke investigated before he retired. We need to talk with him and figure out if the cases are linked in any way. It's very important. The lives of innocent people are at stake."

She paused for a moment, letting her words sink in, then continued: "We won't share his whereabouts with anyone, I promise you that. All we need is his help and his insight into these cases."

Caleb leaned back, studying her thoughtfully. Something about the expression suggested to Piper that he did indeed know something. She just had to convince him to tell her what it was.

"If our suspicions are correct," she said, "then the man we're chasing has been active for a long time, and your old partner put in a lot of hours trying to find him. We'll be helping Zeke find this killer as much as he'll be helping us. Don't you owe *that* to him?"

Caleb took a long swallow of beer, then set the glass down and began turning it in slow, thoughtful circles. Finally, he looked up. "I know where Zeke used to live," he said slowly. "It was a small trailer on the outskirts of the city. But I don't know if he's still there—it's been over five years since I've seen or heard from him."

Piper sat up straighter, excited at the prospect of finally having a new lead.

"But I'll give you a word of advice," Caleb added. "You'd best be careful with him—if he thinks you've been sent by the mob, he'll shoot first and ask questions later."

CHAPTER FIFTEEN

Piper took a deep breath and rapped her knuckles against the weathered door of the trailer, hoping Detective Ezequiel Jimenez would prove friendlier than his old partner, Caleb Parch, had suggested.

It was a convincing hideout, not least of all because it looked abandoned. The siding of the house was battered and dented, the awning over the door torn and ragged, the yard a ghost town except for a few handfuls of jaundiced grass. The windows were obscured by blinds, which were crumpled and bent as if a cat had been at them. In place of tires, the trailer sat on concrete blocks, which somehow made it seem even more depressing to Piper.

"Quite a retirement home," Wade said, arching an eyebrow at a massive spider tucked in the corner of the awning as if ready to drop down on the next unsuspecting person who passed beneath it.

"Think anyone's home?" Piper asked, her voice barely a whisper as she glanced around the property.

Guess the house is retired, too, she thought.

"Hard to say, Pip," Wade replied. "I'm starting to wonder if he's moved on. Hell, we're not even sure if he's still alive."

Piper couldn't blame him for his skepticism. At the same time, however, they had worked too hard to find this place to give up so easily.

"Jimenez might have valuable information, Wade," she said, unwilling to give up hope just yet. "We can't afford to leave any stone unturned."

She knocked on the door again, harder this time. She strained her ears, listening for any sign of movement within the trailer. Silence reigned, and she felt her hopes begin to waver.

"Come on, Pip," Wade grumbled, his impatience growing. "There's nobody—"

"Wait," Piper interrupted, holding up a hand, her gaze fixed on the trailer's window. The blinds had shifted slightly, betraying a hint of movement from within. She glanced down at the empty mailbox and the surprisingly clean front steps. The signs were subtle, but they pointed to someone living here. The only question was whether it was Jimenez or someone else.

"I think he's just ignoring us," she said.

Wade sighed, shoving his hands into his coat pockets. "So what do we do?"

"Ezequiel Jimenez?" she called. "We were just with your old partner, Caleb Parch. We just want to ask you a few questions."

A muffled voice from within the trailer asked hesitantly, "Are you reporters?"

"Not reporters," Piper said. "We're with the FBI, and we need your help on an investigation."

There was a long moment of silence. Then the sound of locks clicking open filled the air, and the door creaked open, revealing an aging man whose wary eyes scanned both agents.

"Badges," he said.

Piper showed him her badge, and Wade did the same. The man studied both badges for several long seconds before gesturing for them to follow him inside.

As Piper stepped into the cramped space, she paused to take in her surroundings. The dimly lit trailer was lined with floor-to-ceiling bookshelves, each overflowing with books on various subjects: true crime, history, psychology, and more. An old record player sat on a dusty side table, accompanied by a stack of vinyl records ranging from jazz to rock classics.

It was clear that Ezequiel Jimenez lived a solitary life, immersed in his own world of knowledge and eclectic interests. Apparently, his only companion was a ginger cat with a missing ear that sauntered up to the agents, rubbing against their legs before leaping onto a nearby armchair.

"Meet Scar," Jimenez said, a hint of amusement in his voice as he observed the feline's antics. "He's my only company these days."

"Quite the character," Wade said, reaching down to scratch behind the cat's remaining ear. Piper couldn't help but smile at the sight of her partner, who would never have described himself as an animal lover, bonding with the one-eared cat.

"Now," Jimenez said, clearing his throat, "why don't you tell me why you're here?"

"Absolutely," Piper said. "Several of the cold cases you worked on involved young women who were found strangled, some of them from out of town. The killer didn't molest them or make any attempt to hide the bodies, which is rather unusual."

Jimenez nodded, a grave look in his eyes. "I remember."

"Did you ever think these cases might be connected?"

Jimenez leaned back in his worn armchair, his eyes narrowing as he considered her question. "Maybe," he finally admitted, rubbing at the stubble on his chin. "There were similarities between some of them, but I could never find any concrete evidence linking them together."

Piper bit her lip, contemplating her next move. Wade shifted beside her, the tall man's broad frame taking up much of the available space in the tiny home. He glanced at her, his dark eyes questioning, waiting for her to take the lead.

"Was there anything about these cases that stood out to you?" she asked. "Any unusual details you noticed?"

Jimenez sighed, the sound heavy with resignation. "I wish I had something to give you, agent, but I don't. If the cold cases you mention are linked, the killer is very careful. I didn't so much as sniff him in decades of investigating."

The silence that followed was uncomfortable, thick with disappointment and uncertainty. Piper exchanged a glance with Wade, trying to ignore the sinking feeling in her chest. The lead they had been so hopeful for seemed to be crumbling away before their very eyes.

"Look, it's been over a decade since I retired," Jimenez reiterated, his voice gruff with frustration. "I've gone over those cases more times than I can count, and I couldn't find a damn thing. I'm not sure what you expect me to do."

Piper clenched her fists, her nails digging into her palms. She couldn't let this be the end. They had come so far, and she refused to believe that Ezequiel Jimenez held no answers for them. She took a deep breath, steadying herself.

"There was some information redacted from those cold cases," she said. "Could you tell us more about that?"

The retired detective sighed and ran a hand through his hair. "Look, I appreciate what you're doing, alright? But I can't help you. I tracked down all the leads, talked with all the persons of interest. Unless you've got something new, you're not going to solve those cases."

He rose and took a step toward the door, clearly indicating he was ready for them to leave.

Piper's eyes darted around the cluttered trailer, desperate for something, anything that might break the stalemate they had reached with the retired detective. She had been so certain that he held the key to solving this case, but it seemed like they were only hitting more dead ends.

It was then that she noticed a small detail amidst the chaos of the room: a framed photograph perched on a dusty shelf featuring a much younger Jimenez standing beside a weather-beaten cabin in the woods. A sudden inspiration struck her as she studied the image, the gears in her mind turning rapidly.

"Mr. Jimenez," she began, carefully measuring her words, "we believe the killer we're searching for is a loner, someone who lives off-the-grid and has a deep distrust for others. He probably has a history of negative interactions with the police, maybe even fines or prison time. And given the age of these cases, we think he's likely in his forties or older."

Jimenez looked at her sharply, an unsettling glint in his eyes. "You know, agent, that description sounds a lot like me. Other than the criminal record, of course."

Piper's heart skipped a beat, and she exchanged a tense glance with Wade. Could it be possible that they'd stumbled upon the very man they were hunting? Her mind raced, trying to make sense of it all.

"Is that so?" she asked cautiously, trying to maintain her composure.

With a wry smile, Jimenez lifted his right arm, revealing a gnarled hand twisted by arthritis. "But, alas, strangling is a bit beyond my strength, so I'm afraid you'll have to keep looking for the killer. I can barely hold a coffee cup these days, let alone take someone's life."

Piper studied the misshapen hand, her pulse slowing as she realized that Jimenez couldn't possibly be their killer. She felt a mixture of relief and disappointment. They were no closer to finding the person responsible for the string of murders, but at least they could cross one potential suspect off their list.

"Alright," she said after a moment, forcing a tight smile. "Thank you for your time, Mr. Jimenez. We appreciate your help, even if it didn't lead us where we'd hoped."

Piper and Wade stepped out of the trailer, the door creaking loudly behind them. The disappointment stung like sand on a windy day, leaving Piper disheartened.

"So much for a breakthrough," Wade muttered.

Piper sighed. "Yeah, I thought we were onto something, too. But we can't let this setback get to us. We have to keep pushing forward."

Wade nodded, his eyes scanning the desolate landscape surrounding the trailer. Piper could see the gears turning in his head, the hunger for answers gnawing at him just as much as they gnawed at her.

As the agents approached their vehicle, Piper heard the sound of gravel crunching underfoot, followed by Jimenez's voice calling after them. "Wait! Hold on!"

Piper turned, surprised to see the old detective hobbling toward them. His eyes lit up with newfound urgency.

"It didn't occur to me just now," he said.

"*What* didn't occur to you?"

"Harold Booth. I didn't mention him before because I didn't want to stir up trouble. He's connected with the mob – used to be, leastways – and I figured that if you went chasing a lead I'd already looked into, you'd just be kicking a hornets' nest. Might even get yourselves killed."

Piper blinked at him, trying to figure out what he wasn't saying. "The redacted information," she said. "It was about Harold Booth."

Jimenez nodded. "That's right. It's sensitive information, given his…unsavory connections, let's say."

"But why are you mentioning him now? Didn't you just say you already investigated him?"

"I did…but that doesn't mean I cleared him. I just never had enough information to make a case, and it was tough to get close to him, given the kind of life he led. But that was many years ago, and that criminal ring has since fallen apart. He might not have the protection he once did."

Piper exchanged a look with her partner, who looked every bit as intrigued as she felt.

"And you say he matches the profile description Piper gave?" Wade asked.

Jimenez nodded, his eyes burning with a fervent light. "To a t. When his bosses got put away, he quit the life—that's how he wanted it to look, anyway. He went off-grid."

"Did he have any priors?" Wade asked. "Any run-ins with the law?"

"Nothing major, mostly petty crimes. But he always struck me as someone who was capable of more. Something just seemed off about him somehow. Something about the way he looked at people, like he was sizing them up." The retired detective's gaze grew distant as he recalled the man in question.

"Any idea where we can find him?" Piper asked.

"Hidden Hope."

Piper and Wade exchanged a puzzled glance. "What's that?" Wade asked. "A hotel?"

Jimenez shook his head. "A commune way out in the desert. Used to be a cult, if you ask me. Town managed to drive most of them out, but Harold?" He chuckled dryly. "It would take an army to dig him out of there, so if that's your goal, you'd better be armed to the teeth—because you can bet he will be."

CHAPTER SIXTEEN

A sense of foreboding filled Piper as she and Wade approached the commune as if the land itself held secrets it would rather not share. Abandoned buildings stood like hollow-eyed specters of the past, their crumbling walls providing perches for wary birds that watched the intruders from above. Ruined vehicles lay half-buried in the shifting sands, their rusted carcasses serving as makeshift homes for the creatures that now ruled this forgotten place.

"Something about this place gives me the creeps," Wade murmured, his normally dry humor absent as he stared out at the forsaken landscape.

"Me too," Piper agreed, her eyes drawn to a child's tricycle, its frame twisted and broken. A venomous snake lay coiled on the seat, unblinking eyes regarding them with cold detachment. She shuddered despite the warmth of the desert morning.

Piper thought back to something Detective Ezequiel Peron had said about the man they were looking for, Harold Booth: *something about him just seemed off somehow.*

Yes, Piper thought. *That's not the only thing that seems off around here.*

Studying their eerie surroundings, Piper couldn't help but wonder if the man they sought had long since moved on, leaving nothing behind but ghosts and memories.

"Let's hope he's still around," she said, more to herself than to Wade. "Otherwise, we've come all this way for nothing."

As they drove further into the commune, Piper spotted a splash of green amidst the desolation. It stood out like an oasis in the wasteland, and she couldn't help but steer their vehicle toward it.

"Wade, look," she said, pointing at the structure they were approaching.

"Is that… a greenhouse?" he asked, squinting through the windshield.

"Seems like it," Piper replied, her curiosity piqued. She parked the car beside the lush enclosure and stepped out, Wade following close behind.

The glass panels of the greenhouse sparkled in the morning sun, a stark contrast to the decay surrounding it. As they approached, Piper noticed that the door was slightly ajar. Taking a deep breath, she pushed it open and stepped inside, Wade on her heels.

Once inside, they were greeted by a humid, jungle-like atmosphere. The air was thick with the scent of damp earth and growing things, and the temperature was noticeably cooler than outside. A complicated system of pipes and hoses snaked around the space, ensuring that every plant received adequate water while keeping the heat at bay.

"Wow," Piper whispered, taking in the verdant surroundings. Having grown up on a homestead, she knew the effort it took to maintain such a thriving ecosystem, especially in this unforgiving environment. "This is incredible."

"Sure is," Wade said, scanning the plants with narrowed eyes. He reached out to touch the leaves of one, rubbing them between his fingers. "But I think we've got more than just some impressive horticulture going on here, Pip."

"What do you mean?"

"Take a closer look at these plants," he said, gesturing to the rows upon rows of identical leafy specimens. "I can't remember the name of it, but it's highly addictive—and therefore lucrative."

Piper frowned as she studied the plants more closely, her fascination with the greenhouse's ingenuity now tinged with unease. "Drugs?" She couldn't help but think of Jim, the man she had chased out the back of Friendly Fred's, and his confession about dealing drugs. He'd been talking about a drug that was made from cacti, but it was still striking, nonetheless, to be coming across drugs again so soon.

"Someone's definitely living here, that's for sure," Wade murmured. "The question is *who*."

Piper pressed deeper into the jungle-like enclosure, Wade beside her. As they navigated the dense foliage, she couldn't help but feel both awed and unsettled by their surroundings. There was something unnatural about this oasis in the desert, a sense of life thriving where it shouldn't. She couldn't shake the feeling that they were intruding.

As they walked further into the greenhouse, Piper noticed a small shed in the back corner. It was made of wood, and the paint was chipped and peeling. Despite the rundown appearance, it looked like it was in use. She could see light spilling out from underneath the door.

"Do you see that shed over there?" she asked Wade, pointing toward it.

He nodded grimly, lowering his hand to the gun at his hip. "Let's see if Harold's home."

Piper approached cautiously, careful not to make any loud noises. She slipped on a wet hose and nearly fell, but Wade reached out and caught her.

Thanks, she mouthed sheepishly.

As Piper reached the shed, she motioned for Wade to cover her. The door opened with a creak, followed by the clatter of metal tools as they shifted against each other. The air inside the shed was stale and musty with the faintest hint of organic matter. The scent of rust and rot hung in the air like a forgotten dream. Shelves held an array of gardening supplies, from rakes and shovels to secateurs and trowels. A workbench in the corner was littered with scattered screws, nuts, bolts and rusting tins of paint.

There was no Harold, however.

Just as Piper realized the shed was empty, a gruff voice boomed from behind them. "Hands up, both of you!"

Piper and Wade froze, slowly raising their hands as they turned to face the shotgun-wielding man standing in the shadows. His eyes were hard, his expression unreadable. Piper's mind raced, searching for a way to disarm him.

"Look, we don't want any trouble," she said, holding the man's gaze. "We're just here looking for Harold Booth. We need to ask him some questions."

The man's grip on the shotgun tightened, but he didn't pull the trigger. In the tense silence that followed, it was as if the greenhouse held its breath alongside them.

Finally, the man spoke, his voice gravelly and tinged with suspicion.

"Who sent you?"

"Nobody sent us," Wade answered, sounding relaxed, as if unfazed by the barrel pointed at his chest. "We're with the FBI, and we thought you might be able to help us with an active investigation."

"Is that what they call it now?" The man snorted. "Investigation? That's a fancy word for sticking your noses where they don't belong. I'm Harold Booth, but I got no love for cops."

"Good thing we're not cops," Piper said.

Harold gave her a long, evaluating stare. "This whole operation here? I've got a license for it, you know."

"Sure you do," Wade said, sounding both reasonable and friendly. "Good thing we're not interested in your plants."

"No?" Harold seemed surprised by this.

Wade shook his head. "Not one bit. Didn't know a thing about this, in fact."

Piper watched as Wade's words seemed to have an effect on Harold. The older man's grip on the shotgun wavered for a moment before he reluctantly lowered the weapon.

"Fine," Harold muttered. "But if you try anything funny, I won't hesitate to shoot."

"We understand, sir," Wade assured him, his hands still raised in surrender. "We just want to talk."

As the tension in the room dissipated, Piper found herself impressed by Wade's ability to diffuse the situation. She was grateful for his calm, disarming manner, especially considering the loaded shotgun that had been aimed at them mere moments ago.

"Look," Wade began, his tone reasonable as he addressed Harold. "We're trying to solve a couple of recent murders that happened not far from here. We were told you might be able to provide some information. Can you tell us where you were last night?"

Harold scoffed, running a hand through his unkempt hair. "You think I had something to do with murder? I don't leave this place. I've got everything I need right here."

Piper studied Harold closely, noting his obvious discomfort around other people, and realized that it was possible he truly never ventured outside his self-made sanctuary. She was not about to take his word for it, however.

"Can anyone confirm your whereabouts during those nights?" she asked.

Harold stared at her, his eyes narrowing. "Do you know who I am?"

"I know you used to be connected to the mob."

"And what does that tell you?"

"Tells me you're capable of anything, including murder—and you'd probably know how to get away with it."

Harold snorted and shook his head. "Well, it should also tell you that I know better than to waste my time talking to Feds. You think that, just because I ran with some young guns back in the day, I must still be living a life of crime?"

Piper's gaze didn't waver. "Are you?"

Harold shook his head again. "I'm done with this conversation. Get off my property." He turned and started to walk away.

"One phone call," Piper said.

Harold paused. Slowly he turned around. "What are you talking about?"

"That's all it would take, and this place would be swarming with DEA agents."

"I told you, I—"

"Yes, I heard you the first time. You have a license. The problem is, Harold, I think you're lying, and it makes me wonder what else you might be lying about."

Harold gave her a hard stare, and his finger began to stroke the barrel of the shotgun. "That so?"

"All we need to know is where you were last night," Wade said, apparently trying to smooth over the tension. "Then we'll be out of your hair."

"Or I can make that call," Piper said, "and by tonight you'll have dozens of DEA agents poking around here. Your privacy will be gone just like that." She snapped her fingers.

Ordinarily, Piper wouldn't have been so adversarial, but she sensed that this was the only approach Harold would respect. If she tried to be reasonable with him, he would just dismiss her. She needed to be firm.

"Maybe I should just shoot you both, then," Harold said.

"You raise that shotgun," Wade warned, "and we'll have no choice but to draw our weapons. You really think you can take us both down?"

Harold's gaze never left Piper's face. He stared at her for several seconds, as if genuinely considering the idea of raising the shotgun and seeing what happened.

Then he laughed, and tension left his body. "You're going to be kicking yourselves when you realize you've been wasting your time."

"How's that?" Piper asked, still wary.

"You want an alibi? I got security cameras all over this place. I can prove, beyond a shadow of a doubt, that I was here last night—and most nights before that. Haven't gone anywhere in…oh…nine or ten days."

Piper's heart sank a little at this. If he was willing to show them proof of his whereabouts the previous two nights, then they'd have no choice but to move on with their investigation.

"Yeah, we'd appreciate it if we could see those," Wade said.

Harold nodded and gestured for them to follow him. They trailed after him, winding their way through the overgrown vegetation until they stepped into a small room at the back of the greenhouse. Harold flicked on a light switch, revealing an array of monitors mounted on one wall.

"I had these cameras installed about six months ago after some kids broke in," he said with a hint of annoyance in his voice. "Thought I might figure out where they came in, maybe sit up one night and surprise them."

He motioned to one of the screens, which showed a feed from the previous night. Harold fast-forwarded through most of the night, going slowly enough that the agents could watch what Harold was doing. The camera caught him walking around in his living quarters, checking on areas of his greenhouse, and then finally settling down to sleep in his chair.

He repeated this process for the night before that as well, and sure enough, both times, he was nowhere near where either murder took place.

"There you are," he said, smiling at them, a hint of gloating in his eyes. "Happy?"

Piper leaned back, resigned to the fact that Harold Booth was not their man. *No,* she thought as a sense of unease coiled in her gut. *Not remotely.*

CHAPTER SEVENTEEN

Almost time, the man thought grimly, taking a deep hit of dream fever. *Almost time.*

The low hum of the engine was barely perceptible, a soothing background noise that accompanied the man's thoughts as he drove along the moonlit highway. The van's headlights cut through the darkness like twin blades, illuminating the road ahead while the taillights of his unsuspecting prey danced in the distance.

He felt a familiar thrill coursing through him, an electric current that set his nerves alight and made him feel alive. He gripped the steering wheel with white knuckles, his fingers twitching in anticipation.

The hunger for the hunt never left him. It was an itch that needed to be scratched, a compulsion that had taken root deep within his psyche.

"Show me the way," he murmured, his eyes never leaving the taillights of his prey. "Lead me to the next sacrifice."

The man's fascination with Native American customs had been an obsession since his youth, a means to escape the harsh reality of his broken home. Over time, he had pieced together a patchwork of romanticized beliefs, weaving them into his own distinct narrative. He saw himself as a modern-day shaman, one who walked between worlds, carrying out the will of the mighty spirit who guided him.

As the man drove, he envisioned the ritual he would perform after the kill: the chanting, the rhythmic drumming, the burning sage—all elements borrowed from genuine ceremonies but changed to fit his own purposes.

"I will cleanse their tainted souls," he whispered to himself, his eyes fixed on the car ahead.

He recalled an encounter with a Native American elder at a powwow many years ago. The elder had spoken earnestly about the importance of respecting ancestral teachings and preserving their sacred nature. Listening, the man had nodded in feigned agreement, but deep down, he'd known he was destined for a different path, one that would set him apart from the ancestors to whom he had so badly wanted to belong.

"Those old ways are not for me," he muttered under his breath, his grip tightening on the steering wheel. What need did he have for customs when he communed with a great and powerful being directly through his visions?

It was during one such vision that he received what he believed to be divine inspiration. In his feverish state, he had seen a great spirit, a fearsome and powerful being that called itself Groll and demanded a tribute to human life. It was then that he understood the true purpose of his life: to serve as an instrument of this deity's will, to guide those it selected on their way forward into the next life.

Groll was not a name he had come across in any literature or heard spoken of by anyone else. No, he was the only person to whom Groll had made himself known, the only one worthy to receive his instruction.

And so, the killings began.

As he followed his latest quarry down the highway, memories of his past victims flashed through his mind. With each kill, the lines between his own identity and that of Groll had become increasingly blurred until he could barely remember the person he had been before the visions started. He felt a flutter of unease at this, but he was too far committed to go back now.

"Almost there," he whispered to himself, steeling his nerves as he puffed on his blunt again. Soon the dance of death would begin anew. And he would be ready.

His heart raced with anticipation as the distance between them closed, the thrill of the hunt consuming him entirely. The night air whipped through the open windows of his car, chilling his skin and carrying with it the scent of sagebrush and the promise of violence. He could feel the darkness within him swelling, growing stronger with each passing mile. It would not be long now before he would strike like a serpent delivering its venomous bite.

Let me be your instrument, the tool in your hands.

As he drove, he glanced in the mirror at the roadside stand he was pulling, and he smiled at the thought of all the passersby who had stopped there, lured by the promise of unique trinkets and souvenirs, unaware that the unassuming vendor was a harbinger of death.

The stand itself was a carefully constructed facade, assembled from weathered wood and adorned with an array of hand-painted signs that advertised the various goods for sale. The stand's structure was simple, with a foldable counter that allowed him to set up and tear down quickly, leaving no trace of his presence once he moved on.

The merchandise displayed was an eclectic mix of items, from carved wooden figurines to vibrant dreamcatchers. Many of these, it was true, were cheap knockoffs rather than the real thing, but that was only a private joke. It amused him to hoodwink ignorant people who had no true interest in his customs or beliefs.

If anyone was willing to stop and listen, the man would regale them with stories and legends, drawing them into a world of mysticism and intrigue. Few, however, held any real respect for what he believed. Others simply rolled their eyes or asked questions just to humor him.

He knew when people were lying to him. There was no mask he could not see right through. It made him angry, hearing those lies, but he knew the cure for his anger. There was only one thing that truly calmed him down.

The highway began to wind through the rocky terrain, and he could feel the anticipation building within him. Soon, he would claim another life, drawing himself closer to the pinnacle of his journey. He could almost taste the satisfaction that would come with completing this latest task.

With Groll's guidance, he would fulfill his destiny—one life at a time.

CHAPTER EIGHTEEN

Piper stood by the edge of the road, staring blankly at the dusty horizon while Wade leaned against their rented SUV, arms crossed over his broad chest. Her brow was furrowed, and she wiped a bead of sweat from her temple. They were both frustrated, exhausted, and utterly disappointed. After chasing what had seemed like a solid lead, they found themselves no closer to catching the killer than when they started.

"Damn it," Piper muttered under her breath, picking up a small rock and tossing it into the brush. "I really thought Harold Booth was our guy."

Wade sighed, pushing himself off the car. "Me too, Pip. But that security footage was conclusive. There's no way he committed the murders."

Piper turned to face him, her eyes intense with determination. "We're missing something. There has to be something we haven't thought of."

Wade took a deep, slow breath. "Alright. Well, let's start with what we know. The killer is targeting women traveling alone in the American Southwest. But why?"

"Maybe it's a matter of convenience," Piper suggested. "The victims are vulnerable, far away from home, and unlikely to be missed immediately. It's the perfect opportunity for someone who wants to kill without drawing too much attention to himself."

"True," Wade agreed, rubbing his chin thoughtfully. "But there must be something more to it. A specific reason why he's choosing these women, in this part of the country."

Piper's gaze drifted back to the horizon. The morning light painted the distant mountains gold, like the columns of a majestic temple. She couldn't help but wonder if the killer saw it, too, if perhaps the lure of the desert was part of his twisted motivation.

"Maybe it's something about the desert itself," she mused aloud. "There's a kind of isolation out here that you don't find in other places. It's vast, empty. Perfect for someone who wants to hide their dark deeds."

"Could be," Wade said, glancing around at the miles of barren land surrounding them. "But why women? And why specifically traveling alone?"

"Maybe he sees them as easy targets," Piper suggested. "They're unfamiliar with the area and have nobody to help them. He can easily overpower them and get away with it."

"Or maybe it's more personal than that," Wade said slowly, his eyes narrowing as a thought took shape. "What if the killer has some kind of vendetta against women, or travelers in general? Maybe he blames them for something that happened in his own life, and this is his twisted way of getting revenge."

Piper fell silent. She knew her partner might be on to something, but she was also aware that there were many possible reasons for the killer's attacks, and they could spend hours theorizing about them. They needed a solid lead, something tangible.

She thrust her hands into her pockets, unsure what to do, and was surprised to find a small evidence bag in one of the pockets. Inside the bag was the turquoise bead she'd found at the scene of Laurel Higgins' murder. She'd forgotten she'd put the bag in her pocket.

She held it up, studying it with fresh interest. "Where do you think this bead came from?"

Wade shrugged. "Probably just a bit of junk left by the victim. Could have fallen out of her van. Who knows?"

"Or maybe it belonged to the killer," Piper mused, her heart pounding at the possibility. "We need to find out where it came from."

"Alright," Wade agreed, pulling out his cell phone. "Let's start by looking up local artisans or stores that sell similar turquoise jewelry."

Piper waited while Wade did his research. As she turned the bead in her fingers, she had a nagging sense that this bead was more than just a bit of junk. It looked unique, perhaps hand-carved, which suggested to her that it was probably very special to whoever had owned it. It might have been part of a necklace, bracelet, or something similar.

"Looks like there's a Navajo reservation not far from where Laurel was killed," Wade said. "They might be able to tell us more about the bead."

The mention of a reservation got Piper thinking. "Is there a map in the glovebox?"

Wade shrugged. "Do people even use maps any more?"

"*I* do. Unlike your precious phone, a map doesn't rely on a satellite." She moved around to the passenger side of the SUV, opened the door, and began rifling around in the glovebox. Eventually, she discovered a map of the area, which she spread out on the hood. She secured the corners with small stones she'd collected from the side of the road.

"If you're trying to get to the reservation," Wade said, "I can just put it in my GPS."

"I'm trying to figure out if there's any pattern to the murders—something geographical that ties them together." Drawing a pen from her pocket, she began marking where the murders had taken place. She started with the three they were investigating, then added a few cold cases Jimenez had been investigating, the ones she thought most likely to be the work of the same killer.

"Like whether they all happened near the reservation?" Wade suggested, taking a gulp from his water bottle and wiping sweat from his brow.

"Exactly." Piper traced her finger along the boundary of the Navajo reservation. "I'm wondering if our killer has some kind of connection to the reservation."

"You think he's Native American?"

"Or maybe he's just using the reservation as a base of operations. Either way, we need more information."

She scrutinized the map, noting that most of the victims – including the three original ones – had all been killed within a few miles of the reservation. She also noticed that they were all about the same distance – roughly five miles – from the outer boundaries of the reservation.

"Wade," she said softly, her heart hammering. "You should look at this."

Wade stepped closer and peered over her shoulder at the map. He let out a low, surprised whistle. "Well, that's something, isn't it? Do you think he's setting some kind of boundary for himself? Like he doesn't want to venture too far away from home?"

Piper said nothing. She was excited by their discovery but also troubled at the same time. If their theory was correct, then they were dealing with someone who was very familiar with the Navajo land. Maybe he was indeed using it as his base of operations, striking out across the desert to attack unsuspecting travelers.

"What does it mean?" Wade asked.

"It means," she said slowly, "we'll have to be careful going into that reservation, because we might just be walking into the lion's den."

CHAPTER NINETEEN

As Piper and Wade's car rolled into the Navajo reservation, Piper was struck by the land's rugged beauty. The late morning sun cast a golden glow over the landscape. Red mesas jutted from the earth like ancient monuments, casting long shadows across the valley floor, and sagebrush dotted the terrain, their silver-green leaves shimmering in the breeze. The sounds of birdsong and distant sheep bells filled the air, forming an ethereal symphony that seemed to resonate within Piper's soul.

"Reminds me of my mom's village," she mused, her eyes scanning the modest adobe houses scattered throughout the reservation. "There's a certain...raw beauty to the land, you know? Makes me feel more connected to my roots."

Wade nodded, studying her. "You miss her, don't you?"

"More than you can imagine."

As they drove further into the reservation, searching for someone to speak with about the turquoise bead found at the place where Laurel Higgins had been murdered, Piper couldn't help but notice the wary glances they received from the locals. Men paused in their work, mothers drew their children closer, and the elderly watched them with narrowed eyes. Though it was subtle, the air was thick with mistrust.

"Hey, Wade," she said quietly, trying not to draw attention. "Why do you think these people are giving us such strange looks?"

He released a heavy sigh. "Probably has something to do with a deep-seated distrust of the U.S. government. Can't say I blame them, considering how their people have been treated over the years."

Piper frowned, feeling a pang of sympathy for the wary faces that crossed their path. She knew all too well the struggles her own mother had faced as an Inuit woman, and it saddened her to see the same pain mirrored in the eyes of the Navajo people.

"It's not going to be easy finding someone to talk to us," she said. "We'll have to be careful we don't push too hard." She thought of the indelicate remark she'd made to the victims' families back at the hotel, and she resolved to choose her words much more carefully now.

As they continued deeper into the reservation, Piper spotted an old woman sitting in a weathered wooden chair outside her home; her deeply lined face depicted a story of endurance and wisdom. There was something familiar about her, something inviting, and Piper pulled over close to her.

"Here goes nothing," Wade mumbled as the two agents got out of the vehicle. The old woman's eyes regarded them warily as they approached.

"Excuse me, ma'am," Piper began tentatively, her hands raised slightly in a non-threatening gesture. "My name is Piper Woods and this is my partner, Lawrence Wade. We're with the FBI, and we were hoping you might be able to help us with an ongoing investigation."

The woman raised an eyebrow, her gaze flicking between the two agents before settling back on Piper. "FBI only come onto the reservation when there's trouble. You'll forgive me for not being excited to see you."

"We're investigating a series of homicides," Piper went on, undeterred, "and we believe someone here may have information that could lead us to the killer."

The woman's expression remained unreadable as she stared at Piper, clearly weighing her options. It occurred to Piper that she was going to have to do more to convince this woman. She decided to lay her cards on the table.

"We wouldn't be here if we didn't have to," she said. "I know what our profession represents to you, and it's not our goal to intrude where we're not welcome."

The woman's voice was hard. "You don't belong here."

Piper studied the woman's weathered face, the lines etched deeply into her skin like the grooves of a canyon wall. She knew gaining the old woman's trust wouldn't be easy, but it was crucial to their investigation. Wade stayed silent, allowing Piper to take the lead.

"I assure you," she said, "we're not here to cause trouble or pin these murders on anyone in your community. We just need help catching a killer."

The old woman regarded Piper in silence, saying nothing.

Piper pursed her lips, choosing her next words carefully. "There's a possibility the killer we're looking for is using your land as a base of operations."

"You think your killer is one of my people?"

"Not necessarily. He could be an intruder, and if that's the case, he's not just trespassing on your land—he's using it to help him victimize innocent young women. Surely that's something you'd want to stop."

The old woman stared at Piper for several more seconds, then let out a heavy sigh. "Ask your questions," she finally said.

Wasting no time, Piper pulled a pair of photographs from her pocket and held them out to the Navajo woman. "Have you seen either of these women?" she asked.

The woman took the photos with trembling hands, her eyes scanning each face carefully. A solemn silence settled over the trio as she shook her head. "I have not seen either of these women before. I'm sorry."

Piper tried not to let her disappointment show. She had hoped for a more direct connection, but she couldn't afford to lose hope now. "That's alright, thank you for looking."

She reached into her pocket again and pulled out the small turquoise bead she had found at the crime scene where Laurel Higgins' body was found. "What about this? Can you tell us anything about where it might have come from?"

The woman studied the bead, rolling it between her fingers thoughtfully. "There are many places where such a bead could be sold," she said finally, handing it back to Piper. "It is not unique to our people or our reservation. It could have come from anywhere."

"Damn," Wade muttered under his breath, his frustration evident.

"Even if it's not unique, any information you can give us could help," Piper pressed gently. "Any detail might bring us closer to finding this killer."

The woman hesitated for a moment, her gaze drifting to the horizon as if searching for answers in the vast expanse of desert that surrounded them. Then she looked back at Piper, something new flickering in her eyes. "You mentioned these women were murdered... How did they die?"

"Strangled," Piper answered softly, her heart starting to race as she sensed the woman's change in demeanor. "Manually."

"Ah," the woman said, her gaze growing distant. She was silent for a long time, long enough that Piper began to wonder if the woman was ever going to return to the conversation. Then the woman blinked and said, "There is a man who lives on the outskirts of the reservation. He is not trusted by our people, and he has a reputation for being…unstable. Some say he has a violent past—that he has attacked travelers before."

The old woman's eyes locked onto Piper's once more, her voice growing firm. "I cannot say for certain if he is involved in these killings, but he may be worth looking into."

"Thank you," Piper said gratefully, her heart pounding with renewed anticipation. "Where can we find him?"

"Head south, toward the edge of the reservation. You'll find him—he's the only one who lives out that way."

As Piper turned to go, it occurred to her that both of the murder sites were to the south, too—which meant that the area where this new suspect lived could be the perfect springboard for committing the murders.

* * *

The Arizona sun beat down mercilessly as Piper and Wade drove deeper into the Navajo reservation, following the old Navajo woman's directions. The landscape was a stark contrast to the icy beauty of Alaska that Piper knew so well. Reddish-brown mesas rose from the flat expanse like ancient sentinels, and cacti cast long, spindly shadows across the hard-packed earth. Despite the dry heat, a sense of quiet resilience permeated the air, echoing the spirit of the people who called this place home.

"It feels we're finally getting somewhere," Wade said, wiping sweat from his brow. "I was getting awfully tired of spinning my wheels, I'll tell you that."

"Hopefully, this lead pays off," Piper replied, her eyes scanning the horizon for any signs of life. She felt a flicker of optimism that they were on the right track at last.

As they ventured further into the reservation, they passed clusters of small, weathered homes, each one bearing witness to generations of family life. Children played in dusty yards, their laughter mingling with the distant barking of dogs. It was a simple way of living, rooted in tradition and a profound connection to the land.

Piper turned left, taking a narrow dirt road that led toward the outskirts of the reservation. The terrain became increasingly rugged, and their vehicle jostled over the uneven ground. They continued driving for several miles.

"We must be close to the border," Piper murmured, squinting against the glare of the sun. "So where is this guy?"

And then she saw it—an old, beat-up trailer nestled among a cluster of scraggly brush and twisted juniper trees. It sat isolated and foreboding, a relic of another time. The trailer's rusty exterior seemed to blend seamlessly into the desert surroundings as if nature itself was attempting to swallow it whole.

Piper's heart raced as they pulled up alongside the trailer. She drew her gun, her instincts on high alert. Years of living off the land in Alaska had honed her senses, and she immediately recognized the signs that someone was living off the land. There were cisterns for catching water, traps for catching animals, and primitive flint tools scattered about.

What caught her attention even more than these signs of self-reliance, however, was the collection of animal skulls propped up on bony branches like macabre warnings to scare visitors away.

"Creepy," Wade muttered. "You think this guy is our man?"

"Can't say for sure yet," Piper replied, her voice steady despite the unease thrumming through her veins. "Whoever he is, he sure is fascinated with death."

They climbed out of the vehicle and approached the trailer together. The hot wind whispered through the brush, the only sound except for the crunch of their boots on the dry earth.

As they reached the trailer, Piper tried the door handle. It was unlocked.

"Ready?" she asked, glancing at Wade. He gave her a nod, and she pushed the door open slowly, revealing the dark interior of the trailer.

The scent of stale air and the odor of decomposition assaulted their nostrils as they stepped inside. They moved carefully, navigating through the cramped space.

"What is that?" Wade asked, covering his nose as he pointed at a bloody object splayed on the table.

Piper stepped closer. "A rabbit, by the look of it," she said softly. "Looks like it's been here for several hours—hence the smell."

"Maybe he already bailed," Wade suggested. "Could have been preparing a meal, then got spooked."

Piper said nothing. Despite the possibility they were alone, she sensed someone else was nearby—waiting, watching. Or was that just her overactive imagination?

Finding nothing of particular interest in the trailer, the two agents went back outside. The sun had climbed higher in the sky, casting a stark light over the arid landscape of the Arizona desert. The earth was a palette of reds and browns, with small trees and scrub brush breaking up the monotony of the barren terrain.

"Maybe he's out here somewhere," Piper said, unwilling to let go of this lead so easily. There had to be some clue as to the man's whereabouts.

Then Wade spoke up. "Over here," he said, his voice tight as he pointed to a trail of blood in the dirt. Piper's heart skipped a beat. She drew her weapon, her fingers steady despite the swell of adrenaline coursing through her veins.

"Stay close," she said, her eyes never leaving the crimson trail as it wound its way through a cluster of small trees native to the desert. The branches seemed to reach out like grasping hands, their shadows sharp and menacing as they stretched across the ground.

"Looks fresh," Wade said, his brow furrowed as he observed the blood that stained the parched earth. "Could be his next victim."

"Or an unlucky animal," Piper said, thinking of the collection of animal skulls they'd discovered near the trailer. Despite this possibility, she couldn't shake the feeling that danger was lurking just out of sight, waiting for them to let their guard down.

As they emerged from the twisted limbs, a gruesome sight greeted them—a body hanging by a rope suspended from a low branch. Piper's breath caught in her throat as her mind raced to process what she was seeing. For a moment, she thought it was human, but as her eyes adjusted to the dim light and focused on the details, she realized it was a feral pig that had been recently killed.

"Shit," Wade muttered. "For a moment there, I thought it was a person."

Piper heard a rustle in the brush. She turned just as an arrow whistled past her face, embedding itself in the side of the dead pig with a meaty thump.

Piper spun around, her heart hammering in her chest as she caught sight of a shirtless man racing toward her with a hatchet in his extended hand. Her reflexes kicked in, and she grabbed his wrist before he could swing down and hit her with the weapon. The two struggled together, their movements frantic and desperate as they fought for control.

As the man tried to wrench the hatchet from her grasp, she managed to knee him in the groin, causing him to cry out in pain and momentarily loosen his grip on the hatchet. Wade grabbed him from behind, wrestling him to the ground as Piper ripped the hatchet away.

"I'll kill you both!" the man shouted, his eyes bulging with fury. "I'll sacrifice you, just like the others!"

CHAPTER TWENTY

Piper paused outside the interview room, steadying her nerves.

You've done this plenty of times before, she told herself. *This one's no different.*

That wasn't entirely true, though, was it? Most suspects didn't come at her with a hatchet, looking as crazed as if they'd been doped up on PCP. The man had nearly shot her with an arrow, for goodness' sake. What would happen if he got his hands on a pen? Would he lunge across the table to stab her with it?

He probably doesn't need a weapon to attack you. If he's the man you're looking for, his two hands are weapon enough.

Quieting these thoughts, she took a deep breath and pushed open the door. The room was sparse and dim, lit by a single fluorescent bulb in the ceiling. At the metal table sat the man who had attacked her, his wrists handcuffed to the table in front of him. His eyes were dark and angry, his posture tense. He looked ready to lunge at any moment like a caged animal waiting to strike.

She sat down across from him, laying a folder on the table. "My name is Agent Piper Woods. In case you haven't realized yet, we're with the FBI."

The man said nothing. His face was a stony mask.

Wade leaned against the wall behind Piper, arms crossed. "We've got all day, buddy," he said. "The sooner you start talking, the sooner we can make something happen."

The man's nostrils flared, but otherwise, he gave no sign he'd heard Wade. Piper found the silence unnerving—there was something animalistic about this man, something that suggested he wasn't entirely rational. For all she knew, he might have attacked her because he'd hallucinated that she was a giant cockroach coming to eat him alive.

She decided to start simply. "What's your name?" she asked.

For a few seconds, the man only blinked at her. Then he said, in a gravelly voice, "Hashkeh Naabah."

She nodded, pleased to have gotten this much out of him. "You must be quite a hunter, given all those animal skulls by your trailer. Why did you display them like that? Are they trophies?"

"They keep the bad spirits away," he said, glaring at Wade as if daring Wade to mock him. Wade, however, showed no reaction.

Hashkeh turned back to Piper. "Why are you here? What do you want?"

Piper took out the pictures of the victims and placed them on the table, facing Hashkeh. "Do you recognize either of these women?"

He glanced at the photos briefly. Laurel Higgins and Brooke Armstrong smiled up at him, forever frozen in time. Then he looked away, shaking his head.

"You're trying to frame me," he said bitterly. "You and your partner over there. Just looking for some way to pin these murders on some poor Navajo man."

"We're not trying to frame anyone," Piper said. "All we're asking is for you to tell us the truth."

"I don't have to tell you anything." Despite his belligerent tone, there was a flicker of fear in his eyes. Piper sensed she was getting closer to a break.

Before she could speak again, however, the door burst open. A young woman rushed in, followed closely by a police officer. As the woman ran to Hashkeh's side, the officer grabbed at her, trying to pull her away.

"My uncle needs his medication!" the woman cried, rattling a pill bottle back and forth.

"Wait a minute!" Piper said. "Hold on, officer."

The officer, a young man whose eyes blazed with frustration and embarrassment, relaxed his hold on the woman and took a step back.

"Please," the woman insisted. "He's not himself right now. Whatever he did, it's not his fault—he has DID."

Wade frowned as if not entirely certain what she meant. "That's the one where—"

"Dissociative Identity Disorder," Piper said. "Used to be known as Multiple Personality Disorder or Split Personality Disorder."

Wade grunted. "We're sorry to hear that," he said to the woman, "but that doesn't excuse him for murder, honey."

Piper thought of something else. "How long has he been having this episode?"

"Only a few hours," the woman answered. "He's been at an in-patient facility the last few days, and he only just got out. They put him on a new medication, and clearly it's not working."

"Is that the only medication, then?" Piper asked, gesturing at the pill bottle in the woman's hand.

The woman nodded. "I promise, after this, we won't be changing his medication any time soon."

Through all this, Hashkeh maintained a glassy stare as if unaware of what was going on around him.

"He's not even Navajo," the niece said in a soft voice. "He just fancies he is, and the elders let him stay out there out of pity. His real name's Walter Plum."

Hearing this explanation, Piper looked at the unstable man in a new light. If she could believe what the woman was telling her—and there would be plenty of paperwork at the in-patient facility, records that, if accurate, would mean this man couldn't have committed the murders – then this was not some vicious, homicidal killer but a lonely, troubled old man. He needed help, not prison time.

"Can I please just give him his medication before he starts up again?" the woman asked.

Piper sighed, still reeling a bit at this sudden turn of events. "Go ahead," she said softly.

Snatching a bottle of water from the table, the niece handed her uncle two pills, then the water. Within minutes, the tension eased from the old man's shoulders, and he seemed calmer, more lucid.

"I'm sorry for the trouble," the niece said. "I'll make sure this doesn't happen again."

Piper studied Hashkeh—Walter—and searched for any sign of deceit but found none. "I appreciate that. In the meantime, though, we'll have to insist he returns to the in-patient facility."

The woman looked ready to cut Piper off, but Piper raised her voice over the objection. "Your uncle attacked two federal officers with a hatchet, ma'am. That's not something we can just sweep under the rug."

The woman hung her head, looking discouraged. Walter went on staring at the wall, oblivious to what was happening around him.

"We'll send someone in to help you make arrangements," Piper said gently. "Thank you for your cooperation."

Piper tried to maintain an optimistic demeanor as they left the room. As soon as the door was closed, however, she slumped against the wall, shaking her head in disappointment.

"Back to square one," Wade said, sighing and shoving his hands into his pockets. "Just when it seemed like we were getting somewhere."

"And we still don't know where this bead came from," Piper said, digging the evidence bag from her pocket. She felt an urge to throw it away, to stop hoping it would lead them somewhere. Thus far, it had only led them on a rabbit trail.

She rolled the bead between her fingers and held it up to the light. She turned it over in her hands, looking for some sort of marking or engraving that might give her a clue to its origin. But there was nothing, no indication of where it had come from or who had owned it—just a smooth, unblemished surface.

It wasn't until she noticed an unusual sheen on the bead that Piper realized the bead was not mineral, as she had originally assumed, but plastic. It was a cheap knockoff—a convincing knockoff, at least to her untrained eye, but a knockoff nonetheless.

She sat up quickly. "It's fake," she said. "The bead is plastic."

"Oh." Wade frowned as if unsure what to make of this. "So what?"

"So," she continued, "this isn't the sort of thing we're going to find at a reservation. This is probably from some flea market or store somewhere. Maybe if we can find out where it was purchased, we can discover whether it belonged to the victim or the killer."

"I hope it was the killer's," Wade said in a low, grave voice. "Because if it was, then we might just be able to figure out his identity."

CHAPTER TWENTY ONE

The sun beat down mercilessly on the desolate street as Piper and Wade stepped out of their car, shielding their eyes from the blinding glare. A dusty wind blew a tumbleweed across the cracked pavement, giving the area an eerie silence that seemed to weigh heavily on their shoulders.

Before them stood a small shop, its faded sign creaking softly as it swayed in the hot breeze. The windows were cluttered with an assortment of trinkets, casting distorted shadows onto the floor like a bizarre dance of forgotten treasures. Its location, which was equidistant from both crime scenes, made it the most likely store to search first.

"Looks like we've found our place," Piper said, feeling a tingling of excitement she couldn't quite suppress. She glanced at Wade, who was already pulling his sunglasses from his face and squinting at the storefront. "You ready for this, big guy?"

"Always am." He flashed her a grin. "Lead the way."

As they stepped inside the store, Piper paused to take in her surroundings. The shop was a labyrinth of narrow aisles, each one crammed with items that ranged from mundane knickknacks to the downright bizarre. A thick layer of dust coated everything, making the air heavy and difficult to breathe. Piper couldn't help but feel as though they were walking through a graveyard of discarded memories, each item a silent testament to someone's long-forgotten past.

"Man, you'd think they'd invest in some air conditioning in a place like this," Wade muttered, wiping sweat from his brow as he scanned the shelves. Despite his discomfort with the heat, his focus remained sharp as ever. "There's no telling what we might find in a place like this."

"No kidding," Piper said, her gaze darting from one object to the next. She felt a strange sense of familiarity as she studied each item as if they were all pieces of a puzzle just waiting for her to put them together.

She was still scanning the store when she saw it, nestled among a collection of cheaply made Native American trinkets: a bracelet of plastic turquoise beads that looked almost identical to the one she had found at the crime scene.

"Hey, Wade, come check this out," she said, her voice barely containing her excitement as she picked up the bracelet. "Tell me these beads don't look the same as the one we found."

Wade's eyes narrowed as he examined the bracelet in Piper's outstretched hand. "You're right," he said thoughtfully. "It's not an exact match, but it's damn close. We should definitely ask the owner about it."

They made their way toward the service counter. As Wade rang the bell, Piper hoped they were finally closing in on the killer. Everything seemed to be falling into place, and she knew that if they played their cards right, they might just be able to bring justice to those who had been brutally taken from this world. Then again, she had felt that way before.

Were they about to be disappointed yet again?

"Let's hope this guy can give us some answers," she murmured, her heart pounding in her chest. "We're getting closer, Wade. I can feel it."

"Me too, Pip," he replied, his voice steady and determined. "We're going to get this guy, and when we do...well, let's just say he won't be hurting anyone else ever again."

Piper's gaze wandered, her attention drawn to a nearby display featuring items inspired by Native American culture.

"Look at this stuff," she muttered, her fingers brushing over the cheaply made dream catchers that dangled from a wooden stand. "It's like they're mocking the culture, turning it into nothing more than a collection of tacky souvenirs."

"Can't argue with that," Wade said, his gaze following hers. Rows of imitation arrowheads and crudely carved stone axes lay scattered on a table, surrounded by plastic tomahawks and decorative headdresses. The items were clearly mass-produced, displaying none of the intricate craftsmanship or spiritual significance of the genuine articles.

"Come on," Wade muttered impatiently. "Where is this guy?"

"Give it a minute, Wade," Piper said, her own patience wearing thin. Piper's gaze fell on a large, ceremonial knife. Just as she reached to pick it up, a sound from the back of the store caught her attention. An old man with thick glasses shuffled out into the dim light, his face a mask of annoyance.

"Don't touch my merchandise unless you're going to buy it," he snapped at Piper, his gaze flickering between her and Wade

"Of course," Piper said, moving away from the knife and returning the bracelet to its spot among the other cheap trinkets. Studying the man's face, she asked, "Have you sold any items similar to that bracelet recently?"

His arms crossed defensively over his chest as he regarded them warily. "Why do you want to know?" he asked, his voice tight with suspicion.

Wade stepped in, inventing a story on the spot. "My daughter's friend bought a bracelet like that one here, and now my girl wants the same kind, even though it's just plastic." He gave a short laugh, shaking his head. "You know how kids are—impossible to keep happy."

Piper watched as Wade attempted to connect with the old man, searching for any vulnerability they could exploit. "Do you have any daughters?" he asked, his tone casual. The man hesitated before responding, his eyes narrowing.

"I'm divorced," he said curtly. "No children. I live alone."

As those words left his lips, it occurred to Piper that this man was about the right age to be the killer. Was it possible he was the one they were looking for?

Wade continued, trying to maintain the facade of normalcy. "Well, if you remember selling a similar bracelet recently, it would make my daughter's day to get one just like her friend's."

"Can't help you," the man replied, his eyes darting between them. "I sell lots of things like that. Now, if you're not going to buy anything, I suggest you leave."

Piper could feel the tension in the air, thick as butter. It was clear he wanted them gone, but she wasn't about to leave that easily.

"I have another question," she said, pulling out the photographs of Laurel Higgins and Brooke Armstrong from her pocket. She held them up for the old man to see. "Have these women been in your store recently?" she asked.

The man blinked at the pictures quickly, then glanced away. "Never seen them before."

"Really?" Piper raised her eyebrows at her partner. "You hardly even looked."

The man clenched his jaw. "Who are you? Cops? Cause you sure ain't just looking for a bracelet for your daughter, so how about you start telling me the truth?"

Piper met the man's glare with a hard stare of her own—she wasn't about to back down. "We're looking for a person, actually," she said, her voice low and steady. "The person who murdered these two women."

The man's eyes widened in surprise, though Piper thought there was something curiously calculating beneath his shock. He took a step backward, bumping into a rack of feathered headdresses nearby.

"Murdered?" he stammered, his gaze darting around the store as if expecting an attack.

Piper pulled out her badge and held it up so the man could see it more clearly. "We're with the FBI. So why don't you start telling the truth, huh? Look at the photographs again."

Reluctantly, the old man did so. After a few moments, he sighed.

"I'm sorry," he said, "but I've never seen them before. I can't help you."

Studying him, Piper had the distinct feeling he was lying. But why? He seemed too nervous, and that made the hairs on the back of her neck stand up even more. What was he hiding?

Something wasn't right here—something didn't add up—and she was going to get to the bottom of it.

"Mind telling us where you were last night?" she asked.

The man's eyes narrowed, and he clenched his jaw. "Actually I do mind," he said gruffly. "That's none of your business."

He leaned back and crossed his arms, his face hard with anger. "Now if you're done here, I suggest you leave."

Piper held her ground, refusing to be intimidated by this man. "Why won't you answer our questions? If you've got nothing to hide—"

The man cut her off mid-sentence with a sharp bark of laughter. "You don't get it, do you?" He shook his head in disbelief before continuing. "This is my store – my livelihood – and you have no right to come in here and shake me down like this."

His hand reached beneath the counter, and his demeanor suddenly changed from guarded to menacing. Piper felt a chill run down her spine.

"I think it's time for you to leave," he said.

But Piper wasn't about to be intimidated. She stepped closer, her gaze never leaving his face. "We're not going anywhere until you answer our questions," she said firmly.

The man's face darkened. Suddenly his hands came up, holding a baseball bat. "I told you—" he began through gritted teeth.

"You might want to think twice about what you're doing," Wade warned, his voice cool. "She's tougher than she looks, and besides, there are two of us. You really think this ends well for you?"

"Listen," Piper said calmly, looking him squarely in the eye, "we just want to talk—that's all. There's no need for violence."

"No?" he asked, his hands flexing around the bat. "Are you sure about that?"

Piper took a step back, ready to defend herself if necessary. She could see the fear and anger in the man's eyes and knew that this situation could quickly escalate out of control.

"Woah there, let's all calm down," Wade said, taking a step forward with his hands raised. "We're not looking for trouble, just information."

The man's grip on the bat tightened, and Piper noticed a glint in his eye that made her uneasy. Without warning, he swung the bat toward them, forcing them to jump back just in time to avoid being hit.

"You think you're so tough, don't you?" he sneered, swinging the bat again. Piper and Wade dodged his attacks, but the man continued to pursue them with surprising speed and strength.

Piper scanned the store for a weapon, her heart racing as she tried to stay one step ahead of the man's swings. Her eyes fell on a costly-looking antique vase sitting on a nearby shelf, and she made a dash for it. She picked it up and hurled it at the man.

His eyes widened as the vase arced toward him. Without hesitation, he dropped the bat and caught the vase with both hands, stumbling backward and falling to the floor, his hands cradling the vase so it wouldn't break.

Piper kicked the bat away and moved toward the man, drawing her handcuffs. "I think we'd better continue our conversation at the station," she said.

CHAPTER TWENTY TWO

Piper sat stiffly at the table, her eyes locked on the man sitting across from her—Elroy Leeland, according to the information Wade was able to find online, no thanks to the man himself.

Wouldn't even give us his name, she thought. *If that doesn't suggest a guilty conscience, I don't know what does.*

The dingy walls of the police station interview room seemed to close in around Piper as she studied Elroy intently, searching for any clue that would reveal his guilt or innocence. She feigned a smile, hoping to appear friendly and relaxed, but every fiber of her being was taut with tension.

Elroy appeared old, his face etched with deep lines like a well-worn map. But there was a strength about him that belied his age. His arms, though veined and sun-spotted, were sinewy and muscular—evidence of years spent working in his store, lifting heavy boxes and crates. These same arms could have easily been used to strangle multiple women to death, Piper thought, a chilling realization that sent a shiver down her spine.

"Look, I don't know what you want from me," Elroy said, his voice gravelly and worn. "I've told you everything I know."

"Have you, though?" Piper asked. "You didn't even want us to know your name."

"Good thing your store is registered online," Wade said. "Elroy."

Elroy gave a sullen shrug. "I have a right to privacy, same as anyone else."

Piper leaned back, shaking her head slowly. "You're not doing yourself any favors here, Mr. Leeland. The simplest way for you to distance yourself from these murders is by being honest with us."

He snorted. "Distance myself? Why should I need to do that if I'm innocent?"

"Are you innocent?"

"Would you believe me if I said I was?"

Piper stared at him, her frustration mounting. This was going nowhere. All he needed to do now was request a lawyer—that would be the icing on the cake.

Wade cleared his throat. "I'm going to grab us some coffee."

Piper nodded, grateful for the interruption. As Wade walked out of the room, she felt her body relax slightly. She had been so intent on finding clues from Elroy that she hadn't even thought of what to say next.

Taking a deep breath, she tried to ignore Elroy's hostile stare and focus her thoughts. What was it he had said about needing privacy? Could there be something in his past that he was trying to hide? With Wade gone, now would be the perfect time to find out more about him—if only she could think of the right questions to ask.

She studied Elroy's face once again, searching for any hint of guilt or innocence that might give her an indication of which way the interrogation should go next. Nothing seemed out of place; his expression remained emotionless and watchful as if he were trying to figure out some sort of puzzle himself.

"How long have you been running your store?" she asked.

Elroy's expression softened a bit, and he looked away for a moment, letting out a heavy sigh. "My father started it back in the late fifties," he said. "I took it over when he passed away about twenty years ago."

"Must be difficult, running it by yourself."

"Because I'm single, you mean?"

She shrugged. "You must get lonely sometimes."

"Sure, I get lonely. And then I remember my ex-wife and how she betrayed me and I'm glad to be alone." He spat the words out like venom, his face turning red with anger. His fists clenched as he continued. "After everything I gave her – my time, my money, my heart – she just walked away like it was nothing. She had no right to do that to me!"

Piper was taken aback by the sudden outburst. Elroy's eyes glowed with rage as he spoke, his whole body shaking with emotion, and Piper thought of the baseball bat he'd brandished back at the store. Clearly, this was a man capable of considerable violence.

"That must have been very hard for you," Piper said, keeping her voice calm even while her body was ready to spring into action should Elroy turn his anger on her.

Elroy looked away again. His hands unclenched from their tight fists, and he let out a long breath.

"Anyway," he continued in a quieter voice, "that's why I prefer being alone. Much simpler this way."

The door to the interview room swung open with a jarring creak, shattering the tense atmosphere. Wade strode in, carrying three cups of coffee in his large hands. He set one down in front of Elroy, another in front of Piper, and then took a step back, leaning against the wall as he sipped from his own cup. The scent of the hot brew filled the air, creating a false sense of comfort within the sterile confines of the room.

Elroy eyed the coffee suspiciously, peering into the cup before slowly removing the lid. As if the steam might contain some hidden threat, he hesitated for a moment before cautiously taking a sip. His body language screamed discomfort like a cornered animal knowing that one wrong move could spell disaster. Piper observed him closely, aware that they would need to tread carefully in their questioning. Pushing him too far could easily send him back into a defensive fury, rendering them no closer to the truth.

"Elroy," she began, her voice steady and measured, "I'd like you to look at something." She held up an evidence bag containing a small plastic bead. "Do you recognize this? Could it have come from your store?"

He glanced at the bead, shrugging nonchalantly. "Maybe. I've got a lot of stuff in there. Hard to keep track of everything."

"Is that so?" Piper said, maintaining her composure despite the frustration bubbling inside her. Elroy's gaze locked onto hers, his piercing eyes searching for any sign of weakness.

"Say, does your daughter want one of those bracelets, too?" he asked, alluding to the lie Wade had spun earlier. It was a clear attempt to provoke her, to knock her off balance and distract her from the task at hand. Piper refused to take the bait, choosing instead to redirect the conversation back to the case.

"Let's focus on the matter at hand," she said. She pulled out the photographs of the two victims, Laurel Higgins and Brooke Armstrong, once more.

"I already looked at those," he said.

"I'd like you to take another look, just the same. We need your help, Mr. Leeland. Are you sure you've never seen them before?"

Piper studied Elroy's face as he examined the photographs of Laurel and Brooke, searching for any flicker of recognition. The persistent buzz of the fluorescent light above seemed to amplify the tension that filled the small interview room.

"Can't say I've seen either of 'em," Elroy finally muttered, his voice gruff with irritation. He slid the photos back across the table toward Piper, his eyes narrowed in suspicion.

"Then why did you get so angry when we showed them to you earlier?" Piper asked in an even and measured tone despite the frustration simmering within her.

"Seems like you're trying to pin something on me. I've had my share of trouble with the law before, and I know how this works. You're out to get me."

"Elroy, we're just trying to find out what happened to these girls. There's no conspiracy here."

"Sure there isn't." He grunted.

It was clear to Piper that Elroy was going to believe what he wanted to believe. She could talk till she was blue in the face and still not convince him.

"Where were you last night?" she asked.

"Where do you think?" Elroy crossed his arms over his chest, his posture defiant. "I was at my store."

"All night?" Wade asked.

"Just about. Left early this morning, one or two o'clock probably."

"Can anyone confirm that?" Piper asked.

Doubt flickered across Elroy's face. "Well, no. I was by myself, like always."

"No security camera?" Wade asked.

Elroy shook his head. "The one I have is a dummy—been meaning to pony up and buy a real one." He swallowed hard, clearly uncomfortable.

Piper leaned forward in her chair, studying Elroy intently. "Mr. Leeland, I think you see what a bind this puts us in. Considering how this conversation has gone so far, I think you can appreciate how difficult it is for us to just take your word for it."

He licked his lips. "I swear, I was at my shop. There has to be a way..." He fell silent, thinking. Then his eyes lit up. "The ATM!"

Piper sat back, puzzled. "What ATM?"

"There's one across the road from my store. I bet that camera looks right at the parking lot. You get that footage, and it'll prove I was there."

Piper exchanged a glance with Wade, who raised an eyebrow in response. It didn't prove Elroy's innocence, but it certainly made him appear less guilty than they'd initially thought.

"Alright, we'll have to take a look at that footage," Piper said, still unsure what to think.

"Does that mean I can go?"

She shook her head. "Not yet. We'll keep you here while we look at that ATM. If everything checks out, then you'll be free to go."

Elroy looked unhappy at this, but he didn't protest.

Piper turned to go, and Wade pushed himself off the wall so he could open the door. Before they could step outside the room, however, Elroy spoke up.

"Wait a minute," he said. "Can I see that bead again?"

Piper hesitated. Then, deciding there would be no harm in showing him, she retrieved the plastic bead from its evidence bag, holding it up for Elroy to examine.

"Ah," he muttered, his eyes narrowing as they traced the small object. "I've seen something with this pattern before."

"Where?" Piper asked, her heart quickening at the possibility of a new lead.

"Another guy sells these knockoffs. He's got a roadside stand he pulls around with his van. A real shady character."

Piper exchanged a glance with Wade, who raised an eyebrow in silent interest.

"Where did you see this man?" Piper asked, trying to keep her voice steady. "And what did he look like?"

"Hard to say." Elroy rubbed his chin, his brow furrowing in thought. "It's been a while. As I recall, he was out near that Indian reservation—likes to hang around the area, close to the highway. Makes sense."

"Sense?" she asked. "Why does that make sense?"

Elroy stared back at her, frowning like she was missing something obvious. "Because of all the travelers going through there. Everyone wants a souvenir, so what better place to set up shop?"

CHAPTER TWENTY THREE

"That should do it," Piper said, tossing the last item, an extra canteen, into the trunk of the SUV. She studied the array of items she'd just purchased from the sporting goods store behind her, satisfied she was prepared for whatever the desert could throw at her.

Wade, standing only a few paces away, stomped his feet and shivered. "Damn, it gets cold fast," he said.

Piper glanced at the sun, which was dipping toward the horizon, its golden light fading into the indigo dusk. It would be night soon—the killer's playground. That meant that whoever the killer's next target was, she might not have much time left.

"Cold or not," she answered, slamming the trunk shut, "the killer's probably on the hunt. We should be, too." She moved around to the driver's side, then paused when she saw that Wade wasn't getting in.

"What is it?" she asked.

He frowned, pressing his lips together. "Where exactly are we going?"

Piper gestured toward the desert. "We've already got plenty of patrol cars staking out the highway. We need to go into the desert, go after the killer rather than waiting for him to come to us."

He blinked at her. "Into the desert? And what, wander around hoping we stumble on him? That's not a plan—it's a gamble."

Piper sighed, growing frustrated. "We talked about this, Wade. We've got plenty of people watching the roads, so there's no need for us to join them. But nobody's looking in the desert, and from what his previous crimes tell us, the desert is his base of operations."

Wade stared at her, clearly unconvinced.

"Are you worried about getting lost?" she asked.

He grunted. "I'm worried about being useless. I'm worried about wasting my time. We can't afford to guess right now, Pip—there's too much at stake."

"I'm not guessing." She found herself growing testy, and she took a calming breath. "I'm asking you to trust me, okay? Can you do that, Wade?"

He stared at her for several seconds. Finally, he nodded.

"Okay," he said slowly. "But we'll need to come up with a plan before we head out there, something more concrete than just wandering around hoping to run into him."

"I'm all ears."

He looked like he was about to say something more. Then his cell phone began to ring—the sound was shrill in the cooling air. He answered, turning away to murmur into the phone.

Piper climbed into the driver's seat and started the vehicle, listening to the low, eager rumble of the engine. She stared into the desert, where the shadows of the cacti and the mesas were stretching out as the sun disappeared.

A few moments later, Wade opened his door and climbed in.

"Good news," he said. "Someone spotted a van pulling a trailer about thirty miles west of here."

"Still there?" Piper asked, her heartbeat accelerating.

Wade shook his head. "He was gone as of ten minutes ago. Still, it's a place to start, don't you think?"

She nodded and put the vehicle into drive. She wasn't going to let the killer slip through her fingers, not when she was so close to catching him.

As she pulled onto the road, her fingers tightened around the steering wheel.

I'm coming for you, she thought grimly. *And I'm going to find you, no matter how hard you try to hide.*

* * *

"How much farther?" Piper said in a low voice.

"Should be getting close," Wade said as he studied his phone, tracking their progress. They were heading for a dirt turnaround at the side of the road where the van had been spotted.

The desert stretched out around them, a vast expanse of sand and rock interrupted only by the occasional cactus or twisted tree. The sun was setting now, and the stars had come out, thousands of pinpoints in a canopy of deep indigo above them.

Piper glanced into her rearview mirror as they drove slowly along the paved road. Her heart was pounding with anticipation as if it were trying to escape from her ribcage.

We're so close, she thought, swallowing hard. She knew there was no guarantee they would find the killer that night, but the thought of him getting away was almost unbearable. She needed this—she needed to be reminded what it was like to see justice served.

And what if he gets away? What will you do then?

Byron Gray's face surfaced before her mind, his mouth split wide in a taunting grin. She thought of the nightmare she'd had and how she had imagined herself wandering into Byron Gray's house, which had somehow transformed into the mouth of a huge, terrible monster. In some ways, she felt as if she was still inside that maw: fighting for her survival, trying not to be lost forever in that darkness.

Wade's voice distracted her from her thoughts. "That's it," he said softly, pointing out the window. "That's our spot."

Piper pulled over and killed the engine, staring out at what appeared to be little more than a flattened patch of dirt marked by a weathered wooden sign that was impossible to read. Piper killed the engine and headlights, plunging them into inky blackness.

For a long moment, they simply sat there, listening. The desert stretched endlessly around them, vast and empty. An owl hooted softly in the distance, its cry as lonely as a death knell.

Piper's heart thudded against her ribs. Somewhere out there, the killer lurked. Waiting. Watching.

"See anything?" Wade asked, shifting in his seat.

Peering into the gloom, Piper searched for any sign of movement or light. "Nothing."

Had the killer already disappeared, vanishing without a trace? Were they just wasting their time?

"He probably got back on the highway," Wade said. "We should—"

Before he could finish speaking, Piper got out of the vehicle. She heard Wade calling her, asking what she was doing, but she ignored him. She needed to see the area for herself, to search for any clues the killer might have left and to try to guess where he had gone.

She stepped away from the car, letting her eyes adjust to the dark until it felt as if she were swimming in black ink. Her gaze swept over the dirt and rock, searching for anything unusual.

The dirt was hard-packed and dry, littered here and there with broken glass and cigarette butts. Piper knelt down and examined the latter more closely, her fingers brushing over the gritty ground. Suddenly she found something unusual—a joint that smelled strangely sweet, not at all like tobacco or even marijuana.

It was still warm.

She frowned curiously at it, wondering if the killer might be high on something.

Could that be part of the killer's ritual? Getting high before attacking his victims?

"Found something?" Wade asked, his boots crunching on the hard-packed earth as he approached.

Piper held the joint up to him.

"What's this?" he asked, taking it. He sniffed the joint, then frowned. "You think it's the killer's?"

"That's the most likely explanation," accepting the joint as her partner passed it back to her.

She stared into the darkness around her, feeling suddenly very aware of how alone they were out here. As much as she wanted to believe they were hunting the killer, she knew they could easily become the prey in this vast expanse of desert night. She shivered slightly and tucked the suspicious-smelling joint into her pocket.

"Too bad we can't just follow his scent to find him," Wade said with a grunt. "If we knew he was on foot, we could bring in dogs. But by the time they get here..."

Piper had stopped listening. She was staring at the ground, noticing something she hadn't seen before. Tire tracks. Shallow but distinct, and they seemed to be heading away from their position into the darkness.

"Look at this," she said softly, pointing to the ground.

Wade bent down to examine the tracks more closely. "Someone's got good eyesight," he said thoughtfully, tracing his fingers along the tire tracks. "Looks like a heavy vehicle with all-terrain tires."

He got up and frowned out into the night, looking troubled. "The question is, where's he going?"

"I think there are two possible answers to that," Piper said softly. "Either he's on the hunt, or he's finished his hunt and we just haven't discovered the body yet." She paused, desperately hoping the former was not the case.

"Either way," she continued, "we have to find him tonight, because if he gets away and sees on the news how close we came to catching him, he might disappear for a long, long time."

CHAPTER TWENTY FOUR

Trentwell's footsteps cracked against the desert hardpan, the sound resonating out into the inky darkness that enveloped him. The occasional distant hum of a passing vehicle on the highway reminded him of his proximity to civilization, but out here, he was alone.

And yet, he was not entirely alone. He had Groll for company, after all, watching over him and speaking to him, guiding his actions. Everything he was doing was at Groll's behest and under his supervision. Without the spirit's insight, he would have remained Simon Trentwell, a mere man. With Groll's help, however, he was something far more than a mere mortal.

He was divine.

His breath came in ragged puffs, partly from the exertion of his pace but mostly from the potent drug coursing through his veins. He had smoked a good deal throughout the day, and now he could feel the fog of the drug taking hold.

Trentwell was barely aware of his surroundings as he moved, his thoughts clouded. Everything around him seemed to blur together, a hazy mess that he couldn't make sense of. His feet faltered as his vision swam before him, and he stumbled forward in a daze.

But then, as suddenly as it had taken hold, the fog cleared from Trentwell's consciousness. He blinked rapidly, feeling more alert and aware than before. He looked around him and saw an unfamiliar landscape with jagged rocks dotting the horizon to either side and nothing but sand at his feet.

How far have I wandered? he wondered, disoriented. Perhaps he had smoked too much; perhaps he relied too much on the potent herb to enable him to hear Groll's voice.

Then, squinting through the gloom, he caught sight of the faint glow of a dome light emanating from a parked vehicle up ahead. An access road branched off the highway, and the vehicle sat in the crook where the pavement met gravel.

There she is, just waiting for me. She has no idea what's about to happen.

Trentwell sensed that the dome light had not come on by the woman's choice but by that of Groll. The spirit had seen Trentwell stumbling off course, and he had turned on the light to show him the way.

The way to his destiny.

As Trentwell moved closer, his heart beating in tandem with his heavy steps, a memory surfaced. Just weeks before, he had participated in a vision quest deep in the heart of the desert. He wasn't Native American himself, but their culture and beliefs had always fascinated him. He'd spent days fasting, purifying himself, seeking meaning among the red rocks and sagebrush.

On the third day, when hunger and thirst had left him weak and delirious, he'd seen it—the vulture. It had swooped down from the sky, its wings outstretched as it circled above him, casting a dark shadow over his prone body. Trentwell had known then that it was a sign, a confirmation of his purpose: to be a guide leading spirits into death.

"Helping them," he muttered to himself, the words slurred by the drug-induced haze clouding his mind. "I'm helping them. It's what I'm meant to do."

The dome light flickered as a shadow passed across it, drawing Trentwell's attention back to the present. He was close now, close enough to see the silhouette of a woman sitting in the driver's seat. He could feel the anticipation building within him, the thrill of fulfilling his divine purpose.

"Almost there," he whispered, a delighted grin splitting his face as he continued toward the vehicle—and the unsuspecting soul who awaited her fate at his hands.

The night air was thick with the scent of creosote and sagebrush, the darkness enveloping Trentwell like a shroud as he moved closer to the parked vehicle.

"Marked by Groll," he muttered, the words escaping his lips in a languid breath. "I'm just his instrument."

As he neared the vehicle, memories of his childhood began to surface, unbidden but potent. Growing up, people had always kept their distance from him. It wasn't because of anything specific that he'd done, but rather what he was—different. Born with a birthmark covering half his face, the cruel taunts of other children followed him like a dark cloud. His parents had tried to shield him, but their efforts crumbled beneath the weight of society's judgment. Isolation became Trentwell's closest companion, fueling his bitterness and loneliness.

"Nobody understood me," he muttered, his voice laced with venom. "But Groll does. He sees my worth."

The drugs he'd turned to for solace in those lonely years had only widened the rift between him and the rest of the world, but now they also connected him to something greater than himself: a higher purpose. In the throes of addiction, he'd discovered a newfound power over life and death, and that power intoxicated him more than any substance ever could.

"Such fragile creatures," Trentwell mused, thinking of the women he'd killed. "So many of them just waiting to be guided into the beyond. And I'm the one chosen to lead them."

He stopped just short of the vehicle, the dome light casting eerie shadows on the ground. A surge of adrenaline coursed through him, mingling with the drug-induced haze in his veins. He could feel the anticipation welling up inside, a thrill that was almost unbearable. This was what gave his existence meaning. If only he had discovered his purpose sooner, how much differently might his life have gone? How much less time might he have spent wandering without purpose, without a goal, a victim of the world's cruelty and judgment?

As Trentwell's foot connected with the edge of the road, the dome light in the vehicle winked off. The darkness enveloped the car like a shroud, leaving only the faintest outline of its shape. This was his moment to strike.

"Perfect," he whispered, the word delicious as it touched his lips.

He crept forward, sticking close to the shadows as his eyes remained glued to the vehicle. But as he drew nearer, something inside the car caught his attention. A stuffed animal lay on the passenger seat, illuminated by the faint moonlight. It was a rabbit with drooping ears and frayed edges that spoke of years of love and wear.

The sight of it sent an unexpected jolt through Trentwell. He felt transported back in time to the days when he was just a child, innocent and unaware of the darkness that would later consume him.

He remembered the days of running through tall grass, carefree and unencumbered by any sense of purpose. His mother had been there with him then, his protector and confidante. She would often take him to the park to play or out for ice cream after dinner. They'd shared secrets and laughter beneath the stars, her voice soothing and sweet like a lullaby.

Those days seemed so far away now, a distant reminder of what it was like before she got sick—before cancer took her away from him forever.

Is Groll really guiding me? he wondered, hesitating for the first time in his mission. *Or am I just a monster?* Questions swirled in his head, doubt creeping into the corners of his conviction. Suddenly the deeds of his past opened up like a dark maw, ready to swallow him whole.

He felt overwhelmed by the guilt of knowing what he had become—a murderer, a destroyer of lives. He thought of his mother and how she would feel if she saw him now, backlit in the darkness like some kind of wraith. Would she understand, or would she judge him as everyone else had done?

Suddenly, from above, the sound of flapping wings broke the silence. Trentwell looked up and saw a vulture soaring overhead, just like the one from his vision quest. Its dark form glided gracefully across the sky, restoring Trentwell's sense of purpose.

He stood up straighter, and breathed more deeply.

How did I ever doubt?

Trentwell swallowed hard, allowing himself just a moment to truly miss his mother before pushing the memories back into their box inside his mind. This was no place for a boy filled with nostalgia; he needed to be ruthless and without regret if he was going to fulfill his purpose.

With one last lingering look at the stuffed animal – a symbol of innocence in an otherwise tainted world – Trentwell approached the vehicle's window. The darkness surrounding him seemed to welcome him, enfolding him in its sinister embrace.

Inside the car, a young woman lay curled across the back seat, her eyes closed, blissfully unaware of the danger looming just outside her door.

Trentwell's hand hovered over the door handle. His heart raced, adrenaline pumping through his veins. He took a deep breath, preparing himself for what was to come.

"Time to guide another spirit," he whispered, and grabbed the handle.

CHAPTER TWENTY FIVE

Piper leaned toward the windshield, her eyes vigilantly scanning the desert as she followed the tracks of the killer's vehicle.

"Where are you?" she muttered, hardly allowing herself to blink for fear she would miss some vital piece of information.

The moon hung low over the desert, casting a pale glow that seemed to amplify the silence. Piper had her window partly rolled down, allowing the warm night air to flow through the vehicle. The sound of the tires crunching gravel seemed terribly loud, almost sacrilegious, in the vast desert expanse.

"he can't be too far away," Wade said, scratching his chin. "We responded right away to that sighting, so he can't have more than fifteen or twenty minutes on us."

Piper nodded, saying nothing. She was too focused on her driving to speculate.

The headlights of her car illuminated the desert ground around them, revealing the occasional cactus or rock formation. The stars glittered above like tiny diamonds, and far in the distance, a coyote howled into the night.

"We're in his world now," Wade said. "He probably knows this whole stretch of desert like the back of his hand. What if he's luring us right into a trap?"

Piper glanced at her partner, troubled by this possibility. Just then, the vehicle jerked to the side as if it had a will of its own. At the same time, there was a sharp hissing sound.

"What's going on?" Wade demanded as Piper fought to maintain control of the vehicle, narrowly avoiding a mesa that appeared on the right.

"I don't know!" she shouted back. As she regained control, she gradually slowed the vehicle. She became aware of a light on the dashboard, the one that indicated the air pressure in one of the tires was low.

"We must've hit something," she said, her heart sinking.

She stopped the SUV, and she and Wade got out. She could still hear the hissing sound, and as she walked around the car, she noticed that the left rear tire was completely flat. She shone a flashlight at it to get a better look and gasped when she saw the source of the problem: a small cactus clung to the tire, its many sharp, stiff spines embedded in the rubber. Piper wouldn't have believed the spines capable of such damage, but here was the proof.

"Well, that explains it," Wade said dryly.

Piper shook her head in disbelief. She had been so caught up in her pursuit of their suspect that she hadn't noticed the small cactus. She ran a hand through her hair, frustrated at this setback.

Cursing under his breath, Wade moved around to the trunk of the vehicle and popped it open.

"What are you doing?" Piper asked.

"There's got to be a spare tire around here somewhere. I'll get it changed and we can be on our way."

Piper hesitated, not wanting to waste any more time. She knew that they were already falling behind in their pursuit.

"Maybe there's another option," she said finally. "We should gather up our gear and continue on foot. We can go faster that way, and the killer won't hear or see a vehicle approaching."

Wade paused, considering her suggestion. "That's quite a gamble. We don't know how far away he is."

"And it's a gamble to stop and change the tire, too. He could use that time to get away." Or take the life of his next victim, she thought.

Wade stared at her in silence, clearly not liking her plan. Then, reluctantly, he sighed. "Alright. But if we're going on foot, we'd better hoof it."

The two agents hurriedly slipped on their backpacks. Then they were off, leaving the SUV and following the trail on foot as they ventured deep into the desert night.

The desert was alive with signs of life they hadn't noticed before: distant howls, bats swooping overhead, and the rustle of unseen creatures around them. Piper's senses were on high alert, taking in every scent and sound.

"Damn, Pip," Wade muttered. "I never realized this place could be so...alive."

Piper nodded in agreement, her eyes scanning the terrain. She fought to ignore the creeping unease that slithered up her spine. The desert animals were not the only creatures active tonight.

"Stay close," she whispered to Wade as they ventured deeper into the darkness. "And watch your footing."

"Trust me, Pip," he replied, casting her a dry smile. "The last thing I want is another cactus-related incident."

With each step, Piper's tracking instincts took over, honing her senses and guiding her forward. She thought of the countless hunts she'd been on with her father, back when life was simpler before tragedy had struck and forced her to grow up too soon. She missed him more than she could say, but it was moments like these that made her feel closest to him. He'd taught her everything she knew about survival, about tracking prey through even the most inhospitable environments. And though he was gone, his lessons lived on within her.

Piper's thoughts lingered on her father as they trekked deeper into the desert night. An eerie calm settled over the landscape, interrupted by the distant howls of coyotes and the rustling of unseen creatures beneath the shrubs. The scent of mesquite and creosote filled Piper's nostrils, mixing with the dry, dusty air that clung to her throat.

"Stop!" she hissed suddenly, grabbing Wade's arm.

Wade froze mid-step, his foot hovering perilously close to a rattlesnake coiled on the path. Its tail shook violently, and its beady eyes glared menacingly at the intruders.

"Holy shit, Pip," Wade whispered, beads of sweat forming on his brow as he stared down at the snake. "What do I do?"

"Stay still," Piper said, her voice firm but calm. She kept her eyes trained on the snake, gauging its movements as she slowly inched closer. "I've got this."

Wade tried to crack a joke – it was his go-to coping mechanism – but all that came out was a shaky, "You know, I always thought snakes were more afraid of us than we are of them. Turns out, not so much."

He began to twist from the waist, reaching for a nearby stick—intending to push the snake away, Piper supposed. That plan, though, would probably just get him bitten.

"Forget the stick," she said in a low voice. "You need to back up—slowly."

"Are you kidding me? It'll bite me!"

"Not if you move *very* slowly. I need you to trust me, Wade."

He took a breath as if to protest, then let it out slowly. Swallowing hard, he leaned back and began easing away from the snake. The snake shook its tail again, but it did not strike out. After a few moments, Wade moved far enough back to be out of danger.

Wade exhaled sharply, relief flooding his features. "Thanks, Pip. You just saved my life."

"Part of the job," she replied, brushing off the praise. "Now, let's keep moving. We can't afford to lose any more time."

The terrain grew rougher as they pressed on, the sand giving way to jagged rocks and treacherous slopes. A lone jackrabbit darted across their path, its white tail flashing like a beacon in the night. Bats swooped low overhead, their wings fluttering silently as they hunted for insects.

"Ever feel like you're being watched?" Wade muttered, his eyes scanning the shadows that danced around them.

"Everything's watching us out here," Piper replied matter-of-factly.

The moon cast an ethereal glow over the landscape, throwing long, distorted shadows that seemed to stretch on forever. Piper's senses sharpened, attuned to every sound, every scent, every subtle shift in the air. She knew they were getting closer—she could feel it in her bones.

Then the wind began to pick up, blowing sand and dust everywhere. In what seemed only a few moments, the windstorm had grown into a full-blown gale, lashing against their skin and obscuring their path with a thick curtain of dust. The vehicle's tracks were soon covered completely, leaving little for Piper to follow.

"Damn," she muttered under her breath, stopping in her tracks. The once-clear tire impressions had vanished without a trace. She crouched down, running her fingers over the rocky earth, searching for any sign of the killer's path.

"Lost the trail?" Wade asked, holding up a hand to shield his face from the wind and biting sand.

"Looks like it," Piper said, raising her voice.

Fear began to creep into her mind, the realization that she might have lost the killer hitting her like a cold slap in the face. She pressed on, stepping over rocks and around crevices as she desperately sought out any trace of a trail. But no matter how hard she looked or how far she went, it seemed hopeless; the wind obscured everything, smoothing over the sand like buttercream on a cake.

"What do you think?" Wade called, a note of impatience in his voice. "Can you figure out where he went?"

Piper swallowed hard, dread welling up inside her. She couldn't turn back, not now. Because if she gave up, she wouldn't just be giving up on bringing a killer to justice.

She would very likely be giving up on a young woman's life, too.

CHAPTER TWENTY SIX

The sand whipped around Piper as she trudged through the desert, stinging her eyes and making it almost impossible to see more than a few yards in front of her. She squinted against the onslaught of grit, determined to push forward.

"Pip, this is madness!" Wade shouted over the wind. "We'll never find anything in this storm. We need to head back to the car and wait for daylight."

Piper shook her head. She couldn't rest, not with a killer on the loose. "He's out here somewhere, and he might have a hostage with him! We can't stop looking now!"

"We won't help anyone by getting lost in this desert!"

Piper continued forward, searching for the tracks. Then she felt a hand grabbing her arm and forcing her to stop.

"You're not thinking straight," Wade said, his face close to hers. "You keep this up and we'll both be dead of exposure by morning."

Piper wrenched out of his grip. "I can do this, Wade! I can find the tracks! I just need a little more time."

Wade exhaled in frustration. "Listen, Piper," he said. "I know you want to find this guy, but we need to be smart about it. If we get stranded out here, we'll be the ones needing rescuing."

"So what do you want to do? Just give up?"

"We should return to the SUV, call for backup. Maybe someone can bring us an ATV." He paused, and his voice softened as his gaze bore into hers. "Please, Pip. Use common sense."

Piper hesitated, torn between finding her quarry and Wade's logical counsel. She knew that heading back to the SUV was the safer option, but she was also certain that every second they wasted was another chance for the killer to get away. If another young woman died because she chose to play it safe, she would never be able to forgive herself.

"You need to trust me, Wade," she said. "I can do this."

He shook his head sadly at her. "And what if you throw your own life away in the process? Would it even matter to you?"

She clenched her jaw and looked away, unsure what to say.

"You're the most stubborn, strong-willed person I know, man or woman," Wade continued. "But sometimes you have to take advice, rather than relying on yourself all the time. Otherwise, you'll get yourself and everyone around you killed."

Piper understood he had a point. But the thought of heading back to the safety of the car made her skin crawl; she wanted to keep pushing forward until she found the killer and solved this case once and for all.

"I get that you know how to survive in the elements," Wade went on, raising his voice above the wind. "It's impressive, believe me. But this isn't about some duel between you and the killer, and seeing who's the better survivalist. You can't let him get in your head like that."

Hearing Wade, a light bulb went on in Piper's mind. "That's it!" she said.

He leaned back, puzzled. "What's it?"

"I don't have to out-survive him," she explained. "I just have to get inside his head and think like him. Where would he go in the desert? What kind of places would be familiar to him?"

Wade fell silent, studying her.

"The Navajo reservation," Piper said. "Maybe he really is using it as a base of operations. It should be north of us, I think."

"Yeah, but good luck finding north in this weather."

Piper tried to study the stars, but the swirling sand made it impossible to see much. Abandoning this idea, she instead pulled out a compass and map. She hunched over the map, trying to protect her face from the wind long enough to figure out where they were.

"Anything?" Wade asked.

Finally, she straightened, lowering the map. "North is this way." She pointed into the distance.

Wade rubbed his face wearily as if unable to believe her stubborn determination. "Alright. But if we don't find anything in the next hour, I'm calling it, understand?"

She nodded. Then a small, hopeful smile crept across her face. "What do you say we go catch this guy?"

Wade grunted. "I'm on board with that. The sooner I can get back to civilization and take a shower, the sooner I'll be happy."

The two of them continued journeying across the desert, buffeted by the wind, and Piper had to squint and hold up a hand to keep from being blinded by the swirling sand. The sand underfoot seemed to swallow their footsteps as they walked, leaving no trace of their path behind them. After some time, as the wind calmed for a moment, Piper squinted into the distance and thought she could make out something against the far horizon—a dark silhouette that was a bit too large to be a rock formation.

"Look," she said in a hushed voice as she pointed. "Think it's a vehicle?"

"I think we'd better find out," he said grimly.

Piper's heart beat fiercely in her chest as she moved forward, and the vehicle came more clearly into view. Its paint was chipped and weathered as though it had been exposed to the unforgiving elements for far too long. The tattered remnants of what might have once been a company logo clung to its side, barely visible beneath layers of grime and rust.

"Could be our guy," she said, her mouth going dry in anticipation. "Let's check it out."

"Be careful," Wade warned. "He could be expecting us."

The sense of danger in the air was palpable as they approached the vehicle, as if the desert itself was holding its breath in anticipation. Piper glanced around, searching for any sign of the killer or his potential victim, but all that met her gaze was an endless expanse of swirling sand.

They drew their weapons and moved toward the van's driver door. The windows were covered with curtains, making it impossible to see inside.

Glancing at Wade to make sure he was ready, Piper grasped the door handle and pulled.

It was locked.

Piper glanced at her partner again, but there was no need to communicate about what to do. He motioned her to the side, and then he drove his elbow into the window, shattering the glass. Reaching inside, he unlocked the door and hauled it open. He reached back to unlock the passenger door, which Piper hauled open.

"FBI!" Piper shouted, aiming her gun into the darkness of the vehicle. It took only a few seconds, however, to realize the van was empty.

The killer was gone.

Piper's heart thudded in her chest, heavy with disappointment as she gazed at the empty van. The stale air inside left them with nothing but dust and frustration. She clenched her fists, feeling the anger bubbling within her.

"Damn it!" Wade cursed under his breath, his face a mask of disappointment. "Where the hell is he?"

Piper shook her head, her eyes scanning the van's interior, searching for any clue that might lead them to the killer. "I don't know, Wade," she replied, her voice laced with determination. "But we're not giving up."

She was about to climb back out of the van when she noticed something on the floor. Something made of cloth. Stooping, she picked it up, then turned on the overhead light to see it more clearly.

Her breath seemed to catch in her throat. It was a light blue headband covered with a film of dust and dirt.

A *woman's* headband.

CHAPTER TWENTY SEVEN

Elana Murray shivered, her breath forming small clouds of condensation in the cold night air. She pulled the thin blanket tighter around her shoulders, cursing herself.

You could be staying at a nice, cozy hotel right now, she thought bitterly. *But instead, you had to skimp, didn't you? Couldn't afford to spend money on something as simple as personal comfort, oh no. That wouldn't be responsible.*

She had seen plenty of hotels along the highway as she crossed the state, but instead of sleeping in one, she found herself lying across the back seat of her SUV, parked on an access road just off the highway. The seatbelt buckle dug into her back like a vengeful talon, and the cramped space forced her to keep her knees bent, unable to stretch out fully. Through the partially rolled-down window, the eerie sounds of the desert – coyotes howling and insects chirping – added to her discomfort.

"Stupid, stupid," she muttered under her breath. "Should've just booked a room."

Elana tried to shift her position, but every movement felt like a new form of torment. The cold seeped through the threadbare blanket, making her wish she had packed something warmer. Her mind wandered back to the warmth of her home in Austin, Texas, where her husband and two daughters waited for her return. A pang of homesickness washed over her, accompanied by a lingering sense of guilt for leaving her family behind.

This trip to Las Vegas, where she was supposed to meet up with old high school friends, had been in the works for months. It was meant to be her first real adventure since becoming a mother, a chance to relive the carefree days before the responsibilities of caring for two children, a husband, and a home became the driving force of her life. But now, as she lay shivering in the back of her car, she couldn't help but wonder if she should have just stayed home.

"Only a couple more days," she whispered to herself, trying to summon some enthusiasm for the reunion. "Just get through tonight, and it'll be worth it."

The howls of the coyotes grew louder, their mournful cries echoing through the darkness. Elana's heart raced as she imagined them stalking closer, drawn by the scent of a vulnerable human. She clutched the blanket tighter as if it could somehow protect her from the wild creatures beyond the window.

"Get a grip, Elana," she chided herself, shaking her head. "Coyotes won't attack you in a car."

But her rational thoughts did little to quell the fear gnawing at her insides. Her eyes darted from side to side, taking in the shadows that seemed to writhe and twist in the moonlight. Her ears strained for any sound that might indicate danger, even as she tried to convince herself it was just her imagination.

"Maybe I should call home," she mused, reaching for her cell phone with trembling fingers. The screen lit up, casting an eerie glow over her face as she swiped through her contacts. "Just to let them know I'm okay…or maybe to hear their voices."

She paused, the phone hovering just above her ear. She imagined her husband's gentle teasing about her impromptu camping trip or her daughters' laughter as they begged her to bring back souvenirs. It would be comforting to hear their voices, but it would also be a reminder of how far away she was from them—both in miles and in spirit.

Would it just make me miss them more, she wondered? Her thumb hesitated over the call button. The coyotes' howls rose to a fever pitch, and she shuddered involuntarily. *No. I'll call in the morning when the sun's up. Everything will be better then.*

With a sigh, she set her phone aside and pulled the blanket up to her chin, willing herself to relax despite the desert noises surrounding her.

"Tomorrow," she promised herself as her eyes fluttered shut once more. "Tomorrow will be better."

The cold desert wind seemed to carry with it a subtle, gravelly crunch that drifted through the open window of her SUV. It was a sound she couldn't quite place—an anomaly in the chorus of night creatures that had serenaded her sleepless evening. She strained her ears, listening for the noise again.

Nothing.

"Get a grip, Elana," she scolded herself, trying to shake off the paranoia that had been dogging her since that afternoon. The memory of that unsettling encounter at the roadside souvenir stand lingered like a bad taste in her mouth. Elana had only wanted to find something nice to bring to her friends in Vegas—maybe a trinket or two to remind them of the good old days. Instead, she'd found herself face-to-face with one of the most unnerving men she'd ever met.

His eyes had bored into her as she browsed his collection of cheap knockoffs, making her skin crawl. And when he tried to pass off the shoddy merchandise as authentic, she'd had enough. Despite his increasingly insistent sales pitch, Elana had walked away empty-handed, the man's dead stare sending a shiver down her spine.

"Stop it," she whispered to herself, rubbing her arms in an attempt to chase away the goosebumps. "You're safe here. He's miles away by now."

Elana shifted her position, trying to get comfortable on the cramped back seat. Her thoughts were a jumble of regrets and half-formed plans, all tinged with homesickness. She missed her family and the familiar comforts of home. But she was committed to this adventure, and she knew she couldn't turn back now.

"Tomorrow," she said again. "Tomorrow will be better. You just have to get through the night."

As if summoned by her very thoughts, the crunching noise came again—closer this time. An icy tendril of fear snaked its way down Elana's spine as she peered out the window, searching for the source of the sound. She saw nothing but endless desert and moonlit scrub.

It's just your imagination playing tricks on you. Just close your eyes and—

Before she could finish the thought, a shadow fell across the moonlit interior of the SUV. Elana's heart slammed against her ribcage as she lay there, frozen in indecision. She didn't want to look up. Maybe, if she just stayed where she was and didn't move…

Fingers scratched at the door handle. Finally, she could bear it no more, and she spun around. She found herself gazing up at a man standing at the window, his features obscured by darkness as he grasped the handle of the door.

Panic rose like bile in Elana's throat, and she screamed as she fumbled with the lock, her fingers numb with terror. She expected him to jerk the handle or even smash the window, but to her surprise, he didn't move. He just stood there, an ominous silhouette against the night sky, the weight of his gaze on her like a physical touch.

Desperation clawed at her insides as she reached for her cell phone, her hands shaking so violently she could barely hold it. "Please," she whispered, her voice barely audible as she dialed 911. "Please let there be reception."

But the screen mocked her with its lack of signal. The line remained silent, leaving her feeling more alone than ever.

Her gaze darted around the confined space of the vehicle, seeking an escape route. Then she realized something that ought to have occurred to her much sooner.

She could simply drive away.

Yes! she thought, scrambling toward the driver's seat. She felt a spark of hope as she slithered across the console, reaching for the keys that were resting on the driver's seat.

Just before her fingers could close around the keys, however, the driver's window exploded inward, showering her with glass. She recoiled, screaming, and when she opened her eyes again, she saw the man's arms retracting through the opening, the keys dangling in his grasp.

She groaned inwardly, unable to believe what was happening.

"Don't worry," the man said, his voice thick, almost as if he were sleepwalking. "You'll soon be going somewhere much more interesting than anywhere you could drive."

CHAPTER TWENTY EIGHT

Piper's hands trembled as she rifled through the van for what seemed the hundredth time, her fingers brushing against dusty maps, spare clothes, and half-empty water bottles. The dim glow of her flashlight illuminated the cramped space, casting eerie shadows on the metal walls.

Wade stood guard outside, his broad frame silhouetted by the moonlit desert landscape. "Anything?" he asked.

"Nothing," she said, shaking her head in frustration. She climbed out of the van and began to pace back and forth, desperate for some indication as to where the killer and his next victim had gone.

The windstorm had finally passed, and the desert was eerily still as if waiting to see what Piper and Wade would do. The headband hung from Piper's hand like a silent plea, begging her to save the young woman from her captor.

"He must be close," she said. "He wouldn't have left his van otherwise."

"But where did he go? There are no tracks to follow, Pip. We've hit a dead end."

Piper didn't want to accept this. Despite her frustration, however, she couldn't argue with Wade's logic. Right now, they had no idea where the killer had gone.

She was about to suggest they start searching the area in a widening circle when a scream tore through the stillness. It sounded strangely muffled, almost like a woman screaming into a pillow.

Piper snapped her head around to stare at her partner, who stood just as tense and erect as she did. Then, without a word, she sprinted off in the direction of the scream, her flashlight beam bouncing wildly over the rocky terrain.

"Wait, Pip!" Wade called out, but Piper ignored him as she bounded forward, adrenaline coursing through her veins. She dodged cacti and leaped over boulders, her breaths coming in sharp gasps. She couldn't afford to lose even a second now.

The desert landscape stretched out around her, an unforgiving sea of darkness dotted with eerie silhouettes of cacti and boulders. Her flashlight carved a path through the blackness, illuminating jagged rocks and treacherous dips in the terrain. The moon cast long, sinister shadows that seemed to reach for her as she raced forward.

Where are you? Piper thought frantically. Her lungs burned with each breath, but there was no time to rest. Sweat trickled down her brow, stinging her eyes, but she blinked it away, focusing on the task at hand.

She stumbled over loose rock, barely catching herself as she skidded through the sand. Adrenaline surged through her veins, pushing her onward. Wade's heavy footsteps grew more distant as he fell behind.

As Piper rounded another bend, her flashlight beam flickered across the access road, illuminating the scene before her: two figures locked in a struggle beside a battered SUV. The woman's scream pierced the air once more.

"Help me!" the woman shrieked, her voice warped by terror. The man holding her raised a hatchet menacingly, ready to bring it down on her exposed neck.

"Stop!" Piper shouted, raising her gun. She fired, the bullet whistling past the man's ear as he jerked away from his target. His eyes met hers for a split second, filled with rage and something darker, an emptiness that chilled her to the bone.

If the man had so much as flinched in the direction of the woman lying on the ground, Piper would have shot him. But instead, he seemed to come to a split-second decision and darted off into the darkness, disappearing behind the SUV as he raced into the desert.

Piper's instincts urged her to give chase, but she hesitated, concerned for the safety of the woman lying on the ground. From this distance, it was impossible to tell whether the woman was injured—or how badly.

"Go after him!" Wade shouted as he caught up to her. "I'll look after her!"

That was all the encouragement Piper needed. She plunged back into the desert's unforgiving embrace, her flashlight beam slicing through the shadows in search of her quarry. She could feel the weight of Wade's trust in her, the responsibility he'd placed on her shoulders to capture the killer. She would not let him down.

The figure ahead was little more than a phantom, appearing only in brief glimpses before vanishing into the night once more. Each time he reappeared, Piper's pulse quickened, the fear of losing him driving her forward like a relentless taskmaster.

But then, just as suddenly as he'd appeared, he was gone. Piper skidded to a halt, her chest heaving as she tried to catch her breath. Her mind raced, her thoughts a jumbled mess of frustration and desperation as she scanned the desolate landscape around her. She couldn't afford to run in the wrong direction, not when every second counted.

"Where are you?" she whispered, her voice barely audible even to herself. With her free hand, she wiped the sweat from her brow as she strained to hear any sound that might betray the killer's location.

And then, as if in answer to her silent plea, she heard it: the faintest hint of labored breathing carried to her ears by the gentle desert breeze. By the sound of it, it was coming from a dilapidated shack only a few yards away.

Her every nerve tingled with anticipation as she approached the shack, choosing her steps carefully so as to make as little noise as possible. She gripped her gun tighter, her knuckles turning white, and tried to steady her breathing. If the killer did not surrender, she wouldn't hesitate to shoot him. She wouldn't repeat her mistakes from the Byron Gray case.

"Give it up!" she shouted, her voice echoing through the night. "There's nowhere left to run!"

Silence answered her, making her stomach churn with anxiety and frustration. The stillness stretched out before her like a physical barrier, and she fought the urge to scream. Instead, she steeled her resolve and continued forward, her boots crunching softly on the gravel beneath her feet.

As she neared the corner of the shack, her heart raced, and she could feel sweat trickling down her back. It was now or never. With a deep breath, she stepped around the corner, expecting to see the killer crouched in the shadows, waiting for her.

But there was no one there, just the empty darkness and the faint sound of her own panting breaths. Confusion and fear clenched her chest like an iron fist, and she spun around, her eyes wide with panic.

"Where are you?" she demanded, her voice shaking. "Show yourself!"

And then, like a specter materializing from the shadows, the killer emerged from the night. He rushed at her with chilling speed, his hands reaching for her throat as he knocked the gun from her grasp. The weapon skittered across the ground, disappearing into the darkness, leaving Piper defenseless and alone.

"Don't struggle," the killer hissed in her ear, his breath hot and sickly sweet against her skin. She could feel the pressure of his fingers digging into her flesh, constricting her windpipe, and fear flooded her mind.

Piper's vision blurred as she fought for air, her lungs desperate for oxygen. But through the haze of fear, she found a single burning thought: she would not let this monster win. She would not be another victim added to his gruesome tally.

"It's time for you to join the others," the killer whispered almost lovingly. "They're waiting for you."

CHAPTER TWENTY NINE

The night air was cold and heavy, pressing down on Piper as if trying to snuff her out. The Arizona desert, so oppressively hot by day, had turned into a merciless void of darkness. She tried to focus on the feel of the coarse sand beneath her fingers, but it quickly gave way to the searing pain in her throat.

The killer's hands tightened around Piper's neck like steel vices, his grip unyielding and vicious. Her vision blurred, stars exploding behind her eyelids as her lungs screamed for air. Panic clawed at her chest, but she forced herself to push it back. She needed her wits about her if she was going to survive this.

"Wa—" she began. The sound that escaped her lips, however, was barely more than a whispered rasp stolen away by the wind. She cursed inwardly; she'd meant to call for Wade, her only help in this desolate place, but her voice had betrayed her.

"Shh," the killer murmured, his breath fetid against her face. "It would be better if you just give in."

"Go to hell," she managed, her defiance choked by the tightening pressure around her windpipe.

"I've seen things, you know," he said, his voice dripping with madness. "When I went on my vision quest, Groll showed me the true nature of life and death. You don't have to fear what comes next. I'll ease your spirit into the other side, guide you to the light."

"Th-that's...crazy..." she gasped, fighting off the encroaching blackness.

"Enlightenment often seems that way to the uninitiated." His voice was almost gentle, belying the violence in his hands.

Where's Wade? she thought desperately. Was he ever going to come? And more importantly, did he have any idea where she was?

As the seconds ticked by, Piper realized she couldn't rely on anyone to come save her. All she had was herself—her own wits, her own strength.

Summoning all her will to live, she clawed at the killer's arms, desperate for even the smallest respite from his relentless assault.

"Stop...fighting," he growled, an undercurrent of frustration in his voice.

"Never," she choked out, her vision darkening around the edges as her body begged for oxygen.

For a fleeting moment, she thought about the woman back at the SUV with Wade. Had Piper managed only to trade places with her? Was she going to be just another of this man's victims, lying lifeless on the ground as he stole into the darkness to kill again?

"Your resistance is futile," the killer whispered, his fingers digging cruelly into her flesh.

"Then...you're...in for a...surprise," she rasped, her words barely audible even to herself.

In the midst of her desperate struggle, she caught a glimpse of something in her peripheral vision. A cactus loomed behind her assailant, its spines menacing and sharp. She thought of the flat tire she and Wade had gotten from running over a smaller cactus... and suddenly, she knew what to do.

With every ounce of strength she had left, Piper shifted her weight and pushed the killer backward, slamming him into the cactus. His grip on her throat loosened as he cried out in pain, the cactus spines digging mercilessly into his back.

It was just the opportunity Piper had needed. Seizing the moment, she gasped for air and launched her counterattack. Her fists flew, fueled by rage and adrenaline, sending the killer stumbling back.

As she fought, she thought not only of herself but of Fiona Taylor, the woman whose life had been snuffed out so cruelly, the woman she'd failed to save. It was for Fiona that she channeled all her regret and pain into her punches. She couldn't get at Byron Gray, but for now, this man would have to do.

The man recoiled, stumbling, his face contorted with pain and surprise beneath the rain of blows. A large birthmark covered half his face, red and livid as she struck him.

Just when Piper thought she had the upper hand, however, the man found his footing and lunged at her, catching her off guard. She tried to dodge his grasp, but he was too quick, too strong. Before she knew it, she was cornered, her back against a large boulder.

"Your spirit will be mine," he growled, drawing a hatchet from a loop in his belt. The weapon gleamed in the moonlight, a harbinger of death.

Piper's eyes darted around, searching for a way out. They fell upon her gun, lying just a few feet away on the ground. It was too far away, however—she would never reach it in time.

The hatchet rose. Then, just as it was about to fall, a beam of light pierced the darkness, hitting the killer's face and causing him to blink in surprise. Wade's voice cut through the night, his tone tense and urgent. "Let her go, you son of a bitch!"

Taking advantage of the distraction, Piper dove for her gun, rolling across the ground and snatching it up just as the man, still blinded by the flashlight's glare, swung the hatchet wildly in her direction. Ignoring the fear that threatened to paralyze her, she raised her weapon with practiced precision and fired.

Two shots rang out in quick succession, their echoes reverberating through the air like thunderclaps. Both bullets found their mark, slamming into the killer's chest and knocking him backward. The hatchet slipped from his limp hand, clattering to the ground. With a final, strangled gasp, he crumpled to the earth, motionless.

Piper forced herself to her feet—she needed to make sure the man was dead. As she stepped toward him, however, her vision clouded. She heard footsteps pounding toward her, accompanied by Wade's voice, sounding distant and unfocused.

Then she was falling.

* * *

A hand touched Piper's throat, and her eyes flew open. She lashed out, pushing herself backward.

"Get away from me!" she shouted, her heart galloping.

Sunlight blazed into the room, nearly blinding her. As the world slowed, she became aware that she was in a hospital bed in a white room that smelled faintly of antiseptic. A brawny-looking nurse stood beside the bed, studying her with disapproval, while Wade sat in a chair, his eyes alert and his hands gripping the arms as if ready to stand at a moment's notice. Judging by the puffiness of his eyes, Piper guessed he had been sleeping before her shout woke him.

"Are you finished?" the nurse asked, arching an eyebrow. "I was just checking the bandage on your throat."

Puzzled, Piper touched her throat and felt a thin strip of fabric covering the skin. She winced at the pressure, and her mind flashed back to the night before. The hatchet, the flashlight, the sound of Wade's voice...

"What happened?" she asked, her words muffled slightly as she tried to speak around the bandage.

"You don't remember?" Wade asked, rising and approaching the bed.

Piper shook her head slowly. "Not all the details."

"You were attacked," he said gently. "By the man we were trying to find. You gave as good as you got, though."

Piper's fingers strayed back to her throat, exploring its tenderness gingerly. She closed her eyes against a wave of dizziness and nausea—the memory of that moment was still vivid in her mind's eye: the gleam of the moonlight on the blade of that deadly hatchet, and then Wade's face illuminated by flashlight as he raced toward them both...

She threw back the sheet and slipped her feet to the floor. She wanted – no, *needed* – to get back to work, to ensure that no other innocents would suffer at the hands of men like the one she'd killed.

"Slow down," Wade said, grabbing hold of her to support her. He gave the nurse a worried glance. "Is she okay to leave?"

The nurse let out an overtaxed sigh. "Her vitals are good. She just needs rest."

Piper looked at her partner. "I'm fine, Wade. Really."

He gave her a long, evaluating look. Then he shrugged. "Okay," he finally said. "But when you get home, you're going straight to bed. Deal?"

"Deal."

Piper noticed a small pile of clothing on the stand beside the bed. Women's clothing, but not the ones she'd been wearing the previous night.

"I took the liberty of picking you up a new set of clothes," Wade said, sounding a bit sheepish. "I hope they fit."

Piper gave him a small smile. "You never cease to amaze, do you?"

Wade shrugged and followed the nurse out of the room. "Just let me know when you're ready," he said before closing the door.

Piper slipped into the new clothes, which fit surprisingly well. She was impressed—Wade had even picked clothes that matched her personal style. She ran her fingers down the soft cotton fabric, admiring the way it clung to her curves. It was almost as if Wade had a sixth sense when it came to understanding what she liked.

As she finished dressing, Piper couldn't help but feel a spark of something in her chest—admiration? Affection? Whatever it was, it felt warm and comforting. She supposed it would have seemed romantic if she weren't so tired.

She stepped out into a sun-drenched hallway, where Wade waited with his hands in his pockets, looking like he belonged there. He smiled when their eyes met, and Piper couldn't help but smile back. There was something undeniably comforting about being around him.

As they walked down the sterile hospital corridor, Wade broke the silence. "I spoke to Elena earlier, the woman we helped rescue. She's safe and unharmed, thanks to you. She wanted me to pass along her gratitude."

Piper smiled weakly, feeling a weight lift from her chest. "I'm glad she's okay. This whole thing has been a nightmare."

"Tell me about it," Wade agreed, his voice heavy with emotion. They reached the waiting area and paused for a moment, the sunlight streaming in through the large windows casting a warm glow on their faces.

The conversation stilled as they both stood there, lost in their thoughts. Piper felt Wade's eyes on her, and when she met his gaze, she saw a vulnerability she hadn't expected.

"Pip," he said softly. "I was so worried about you. When I found you out there, fighting for your life..." He shook his head. "I've never been that scared before."

His voice was raw, full of emotion that made Piper's stomach flutter with a mixture of nervousness and affection. She knew he cared for her, but hearing him admit it like this – in such an open, vulnerable way – made her realize just how deep his feelings went. And she couldn't deny that she felt the same pull toward him, a magnetic attraction that seemed to grow stronger the more time they spent together.

"Thank you, Wade," she whispered, her eyes shining with unshed tears. "For everything."

He stepped closer to her, his large frame radiating warmth and comfort. The air between them seemed to crackle with electricity as he gently cupped her face in his hands. "I'll always be there for you, Pip. No matter what."

Their lips met in a tender kiss that seemed to last an eternity. It was a sweet, gentle moment that held the promise of something more, and yet Piper couldn't shake the feeling that it was also somehow wrong—

that the timing, or the circumstances, or maybe just her own jumbled emotions were making the whole thing feel like a mistake.

As they pulled apart, breathless and slightly dazed, Piper tried to push away her doubts. She knew that she and Wade had something special, something worth exploring. But for now, they had other things to focus on—like healing and moving on from the horrors of the previous night.

She cleared her throat. "What do you say we get out of here?"

He nodded, his eyes shining. "That sounds like a great idea."

As they stepped into the parking lot, the Arizona sun warmed Piper's face, providing a small measure of comfort after the chill of the hospital. She squinted against the brightness, searching for Wade's car among the sea of vehicles.

"Over here," he called, leading her to a spot near the edge of the lot. As they approached his car, Piper couldn't help but notice how their conversation had dwindled to almost nothing since leaving her hospital room. The easy banter they usually shared was conspicuously absent, replaced by a palpable tension that seemed to vibrate between them.

They both climbed into the car. Wade started the engine and stared through the windshield. "So, uh…what now?"

"The airport," she said simply. "It's time to go home."

CHAPTER THIRTY

Piper Woods stood at the window of her Alaskan cabin, watching snowflakes dance and swirl in the icy wind. The cold numbed the pain in her throat, where Trentwell's fingers had dug in with a deadly force just days ago.

She shivered, recalling how close she had come to death.

She turned away from the window and busied herself with tidying up, folding laundry and rearranging items on the shelves. Her hands needed something to do, anything to keep her mind from drifting back to the case.

She moved toward the stove and started preparing fish for her meal, slicing through the flesh with practiced precision. The scent of the fresh catch filled the air, a simple pleasure she'd grown to appreciate during her time in Alaska.

As she worked, her thoughts couldn't help but wander back to the fight in the desert. The image of Trentwell's shocked face as she pulled the trigger haunted her. She was no stranger to the darker aspects of her job, but taking a life still left her feeling hollow and unsettled.

Piper shook her head, trying to dispel the memory. It had been necessary, she reminded herself. Trentwell would have killed her without any hesitation. But knowing that didn't make it any easier.

Just then, Piper caught a glimpse of movement outside the window. Squinting against the snow, she saw a figure trudging determinedly toward her cabin. As the figure drew closer, she recognized the unmistakable build of Lawrence Wade.

A mix of excitement and confusion bubbled within her. What could have brought him all the way out here?

As Wade approached, Piper couldn't help but be reminded of the kiss they'd shared at the hospital mere days ago. The memory stirred a confusing cocktail of emotions within her—warmth and affection but also uncertainty. She wasn't sure what she wanted from their relationship or where they stood now.

She hurried to the door, opening it just as Wade was about to knock.

"Hey, Pip," he said a bit uncertainly, snowflakes clinging to his eyebrows. "Remember me?"

For a moment, she could only stare at him, hardly believing he was there. Again. Then she recovered herself and stepped aside, gesturing for him to come in.

Piper kept her back to Wade, busying herself with the kettle while she composed herself. She felt a strange mixture of emotions at his presence in the cabin with her.

"Never thought I'd see you up here again so soon," she said without looking at him. "You must have a good reason to brave the cold."

Wade chuckled, rubbing his hands together to ward off the chill. "You know me too well, Pip. But first things first, let's get warmed up. You got any coffee?"

"Just tea. I know how much you liked it last time." She smiled at him.

Wade grunted and, waving a hand to decline the tea, sat down in a chair. He took a deep breath as if reluctant to share what he had come to say.

What could this be about? Piper wondered, feeling suddenly uneasy.

"I've got some news for you," he finally said, then paused, staring her in the eye. "It's about your mother."

Piper's heart skipped a beat at the mention of her long-lost mother. Was it possible that Wade had found new information about her? She felt a mix of hope and trepidation, unsure if she was ready to hear what he had to say.

"I've done some digging over the past few days," he continued, his voice serious. "I managed to hack into the National Park Service database, and—"

"You did *what*?" She sat forward, hardly able to believe what she was hearing.

"And I found something interesting," he continued. "A citation for illegally camping on federal land. The name on the citation: Ila Woods."

Piper's breath caught in her throat. Could it really be her mother? Alive, after all these years?

"The date on the citation confirms it," Wade added softly. "She's still out there, Pip."

Tears welled in Piper's eyes as she tried to process the information. Gratitude toward Wade for risking his career to find this for her mingled with the shock of learning her mother was still alive. "Thank you, Wade," she whispered. "I don't know how I can ever repay you."

Wade shifted in his seat, his large frame making the cabin's furniture seem comically small. He stared at his hands as if searching them for answers. A few moments passed before he finally spoke, his voice hesitant.

"Actually, there *is* something you could do for me, Pip," he said. "I came here for another reason, too. The FBI brass want to meet with you again. They really want you back, full time."

Piper frowned, her heart racing as she considered the implications. Inwardly, she was reluctant to get involved with the Bureau again—it had cost her so much already. But she knew she owed Wade for the sacrifices he'd made to help her find her mother. Could she really refuse him after what he'd just shared with her?

"I understand your reluctance," Wade said. "You made it very clear before why you didn't want to come back." He leaned forward, staring earnestly into her eyes. "But we need help on some big cases right now—the kind of cases that only someone with your skill set can handle. It's important work, and it will make a difference." Then he added, with a mischievous grin, "Plus it pays surprisingly well."

Piper sighed, her mind still reeling from the news of her mother. She hated to admit it, but Wade was right—she did have a skill set that could be put to good use. And while she was hesitant to make any decisions now, in this moment of revelation and confusion, she found herself nodding slowly in agreement.

"Alright," she said softly. "I'll take the meeting. I can't make any promises as to the outcome, though."

Wade's face brightened. Then he let out a low, soft chuckle. "Well, Pip, I don't know whether to thank you or apologize for dragging you back into the FBI's clutches."

Piper managed a small smile, appreciating her partner's attempt to lighten the mood. "Better whisk me away before I can change my mind."

Wade pulled himself from his seat. "Already got a chopper waiting. How long will it take you to pack?"

"Just a few minutes. It's not like there's much I could bring, even if I wanted to."

Wade nodded, looking around. "Alright, well, I'll step outside and give you some space. But don't leave me freezing out there for long, okay?"

She smiled. "Wouldn't dream of it."

She watched Wade leave the cabin, closing the door behind him. Then she set about packing for the trip.

And all the while, memories of past failures circled her like vultures.

* * *

Well, this is a bit of a culture shock, Piper thought, the plush carpet beneath her feet seeming to swallow her steps as she followed Wade into the opulent conference room.

The grand chandelier overhead cast a warm glow over the polished mahogany table, and Piper couldn't help but feel out of place in the luxurious surroundings. Her fingers absently traced the scratches on her throat, a souvenir from her fight with Trentwell, and she felt a familiar twinge of nostalgia as she thought about her home back in Alaska.

The three men at the table were all immaculately dressed, and they spoke in hushed tones, casting curious glances in her direction as she and Wade approached. She wasn't one to easily get intimidated by powerful people, but this time it was different—this place felt so alien to her. She took a deep breath to steady herself as her former boss, Doug Maxwell, rose and extended his hand.

"Glad you could join us," he said, smiling formally as he shook hands with Piper and Wade. "Please, have a seat." He gestured toward the high-backed chairs that surrounded the table. Piper hesitated for a moment before taking a seat beside Wade, who gently bumped her knee with his under the table, a friendly reminder that he was on her side.

In the few seconds of silence that followed, Piper tugged at the collar of her borrowed blouse, the material itching against her skin like a foreign invader. She longed for the comfort of her cabin, the softness of her worn flannel shirts, and the simple familiarity of her surroundings. All of that, however, would have to wait.

"Alright, let's get started," Maxwell said, adjusting his tie and clearing his throat. "We appreciate you coming here today, Miss Woods. As you know, we've been very impressed by your work on the Trentwell case, and we believe there are many more cases out there that could benefit from your unique skill set."

Piper shifted in her seat, feeling the eyes of the room fixed on her as if she were a specimen under a microscope.

"Here's the thing," Maxwell continued, leaning forward and clasping his hands together on the table. "We want you to reconsider your refusal to join the Bureau full time again. You're exceptionally good at what you do, Piper, and there are innocent people out there who need your help."

The room was silent; the only sound was the hum of the air conditioning overhead.

"I hardly need to explain the benefits," he continued. "You'll have the opportunity to travel, to make a difference in others' lives—-and the salary won't hurt, either." He glanced at the two men beside him, who chuckled politely.

Piper's thoughts swirled like a whirlwind, her stomach tying itself into knots. She knew that Wade had brought her here because he believed it was the right thing for her, but the thought of returning to the Bureau still filled her with unease. Was this really the right decision?

"We've updated our benefits package, too," Maxwell continued. "We are prepared to offer you—"

"Alright," Piper said before Maxwell could finish his pitch. The word hung in the air like a delicate snowflake, drawing the attention of everyone in the room.

"Excuse me?" Maxwell blinked in surprise, his mouth left slightly agape.

"I said alright," Piper repeated, her voice steadier and more resolute this time. "I'll come back."

"Really?" Wade asked, his face a mix of shock and concern. He leaned in closer, his voice low and urgent. "Are you sure about this, Pip? You don't have to do this if you don't want to."

It was clear that, as much as Wade wanted her to come back, he hadn't really thought she would, at least not without extensive convincing. He didn't seem to know what to make of this sudden capitulation.

But Piper held her ground, locking eyes with her partner. She had made up her mind, and she wasn't going to change it now.

"I'm sure, Wade," she replied with conviction. "Let's do this."

As the men in suits exchanged glances and murmured amongst themselves, Piper felt the first stirrings of anticipation. For better or worse, she was taking control of her life once more. The realization was both exhilarating and terrifying.

"Well," Maxwell said, still looking puzzled, "I'm very happy to hear that. I have to admit, I'm a bit surprised, considering your past stance. But there's no need to focus on that now. How soon can you begin?"

"How about today?"

Maxwell looked even more puzzled than before. Then, as if not wanting her to change her mind, he recovered and said, "Fantastic! We'll start right away. There's some paperwork to fill out, of course, but we'll have you working on another investigation in no time." He smiled, then rose and shook her hand once more.

"You made the right choice," he said.

Piper smiled back. "Yes, I believe I did."

The conference room emptied out like water down a drain, leaving only Wade and Piper standing amongst the expensive leather chairs and polished mahogany table. The afternoon sun filtered in through the tall windows, casting long shadows on the plush carpet.

"Alright, Pip," Wade said, breaking the silence that had settled over them. He leaned back against the table, his strong arms crossed over his broad chest. "You've got to tell me what changed your mind."

Piper turned to face him, taking in the concern etched across his features. She knew she owed him an explanation, but she couldn't bring herself to reveal the whole truth just yet.

"You did," she said simply, offering him a small smile. "I trust you, Wade. And if you think it's the right thing for me to do, then I'm willing to give it a shot."

Wade frowned slightly, clearly not satisfied with her answer. He knew her well enough to sense when something was off, and he wasn't going to let her off the hook that easily.

"Come on, Pip," he pressed gently. "You were so adamant about staying away from the Bureau before. What really changed?"

Piper hesitated, her gaze drifting to the floor as she tried to formulate an answer that would satisfy him without revealing too much.

"Sometimes, we have to make sacrifices for the greater good," she said finally, looking back up at him. "And maybe...maybe there are things I can accomplish by being part of the FBI again. Things that are bigger than myself."

His dark eyes searched hers as if unsure what to make of this answer.

"I want," she began, then reconsidered and started over. "I *need* to do some good in the world, Wade. And maybe the FBI is the best way for me to do that."

Wade studied her for a moment longer before nodding slowly, accepting her words at face value. "Alright, Pip," he said. "If this is really what you want, then I'll support you every step of the way. You know that, right?"

Piper smiled warmly at him, touched by his unwavering loyalty. "I know, Wade," she replied, reaching out to squeeze his hand. "And thank you. For everything."

"Hey," he said, returning the gesture with a firm grip. "That's what partners are for, right?"

She knew that joining the FBI again would bring its own set of challenges, but she was ready. She'd had a whole year to prepare, after all.

"Come on," Wade said, releasing her hand and gesturing toward the door. "Let's get out of here and celebrate your big decision."

"Sounds like a plan," Piper agreed, allowing herself to be swept up in the moment. She would worry about the consequences of her choices later; for now, she would focus on the good she could do and the hope that she might finally find the answers she'd been searching for.

Because, despite what she'd told Wade, she wasn't just coming back to do some good in the world. That was part of it, sure, but even more than that, she was returning to the Bureau for the mother she had lost for so many years, the mother who was apparently still out there.

And she was going to use the Bureau's resources to find her.

EPILOGUE

Professor Gauther stood at the front of the college lecture hall, his mouth lecturing on sociology while his eyes endeavored not to stare at the brunette sitting in the second row.

Brenda, he thought. *Sweet, innocent Brenda.*

Her face was enchantingly symmetrical, her high cheekbones and full lips framed by long, dark hair. He tried to force himself to look at the other students, to focus on the words coming out of his mouth, but it felt like an impossible task.

"Social mobility," he was saying, "is the extent to which individuals can change their social status within a society. It can be affected by a variety of factors, such as education and employment opportunities."

His gaze drifted down to her slender hands, curled around the edge of her desk. He wondered what it would feel like to hold them on his own. To grasp them.

"Class divisions that impede social mobility are still prevalent in many societies today," he continued, "which can lead to increased inequality among individuals."

He noticed the way she sat straighter when he glanced in her direction, head tilted slightly, and eyes focused intently on him. Was she drawn to him the way he was drawn to her? Was there some special force uniting them, some thread of destiny?

He wished he could continue the lecture if only to keep her attention captive longer, but a quick look at the clock told him his time was up.

"That's all for today," he said, his words followed by the immediate rustle of backpacks and laptop cases as students began packing up. "But remember, the next paper is due on Friday. I want originality and clarity. No BS."

The students hurried out, eager for the freedom of lunchtime or the chance to meet up with friends. Brenda, however, lingered, chatting with a small group near the door. Gauther pretended to shuffle papers on his desk, periodically glancing up to observe her.

As she prepared to leave with her friends, he seized the opportunity.

"Ah, Brenda," he called out, his voice casual yet firm. "May I have a word with you, please?"

She looked surprised, her eyebrows knitting together in slight concern. Her friends exchanged glances before moving on without her, leaving her alone in the now-empty room.

"Is everything okay?" she asked hesitantly, clutching her books to her chest. "I'm not in trouble, am I?"

The professor smiled warmly, attempting to put her at ease. "No, no, not at all," he said, gesturing for her to approach his desk. "I just wanted to talk about the last paper you turned in."

Brenda's face flushed with a mix of relief and embarrassment as she made her way to the front of the room, her heels clicking on the linoleum floor. The professor watched her closely, trying to suppress the thrill that coursed through him at the thought of having her undivided attention.

"I know you try very hard, Brenda," he began, leaning back against the edge of his desk. "But I have to admit, your last paper left me somewhat…disappointed." He paused, studying her reaction. "I believe you can do much better."

"I-I'm sorry," she stammered, her eyes downcast. "I'll do better next time, I promise."

"See that you do," he said, his eyes lingering on the curve of her cheek, the graceful line of her neck. "I think some tutoring might be just what you need to correct these mistakes and truly excel in this course."

"Would *you* be willing to tutor me?" she asked suddenly, her gaze locked onto his. There was something almost pleading in her eyes, a vulnerability that tugged at something deep within him.

"Ah, well," he hesitated, feigning reluctance even as his heart leaped at the prospect of spending more time with her. "I am quite busy these days, you understand. Between my research and other commitments, I have very little free time."

"Please," she pressed. "I really need your help. I don't want to disappoint you again."

Her words struck a chord within him, an unspoken desire that had been lurking just beneath the surface since their first encounter. Still, he couldn't give in too easily.

He took a reluctant breath that hissed along his teeth. "I don't know. I've got a lot of irons in the fire just now, and I wouldn't want to be seen showing favoritism."

She touched her arm again. "Please, Professor Gauther. It would mean so much."

Glancing at his wristwatch, Gauther's eyes flickered with a sudden realization. "You know what, Brenda? It appears I have some time right now. We could sit down in one of the conference rooms and go over your paper, if you'd like."

Brenda hesitated, her gaze shifting to the floor. "Well, I was supposed to hang out with some friends...but if you really think it would help..."

"Trust me," he said firmly, his voice betraying a hint of urgency. "If we don't do this now, it'll be several days before we can find another opportunity. And if your next paper doesn't show marked improvement, you might flunk the class."

She bit her lip, torn between her commitment to her friends and the need to improve her academic standing. Gauther watched her carefully, his heart pounding in anticipation. He willed her to choose him, to prioritize their time together.

"Alright," she finally relented, her voice soft and hesitant. "I suppose I can reschedule with my friends."

"Excellent decision," he said, trying to mask his relief. "There's not a moment to lose."

Gauther led Brenda through the quiet halls of the college, heading toward the conference rooms. As they walked, he noticed the way her hair caught the light, the elegant curve of her neck, and the delicate arch of her brow. All these details only served to reinforce his obsession with her symmetrical beauty.

As they rounded a corner, Gauther caught sight of a group of students up ahead, their voices bubbling with laughter and camaraderie. Wanting to avoid between seen with Brenda, he suddenly changed course, pulling Brenda toward a wing of the college that was currently under renovation.

"Where are we going?" she asked, her brow furrowing with uncertainty.

"Trust me, it's a shortcut," he said, flashing her a reassuring smile. She didn't seem to entirely believe him, but she made no protest.

Gauther opened the door, revealing a hallway under construction: the carpet had been torn up, revealing the cold concrete beneath, and the plaster had been removed from the walls on either side. Dust motes danced in the dim light that filtered through the grimy windows, casting a sickly glow across the obstacles littering the floor: hand tools, extension cords, and stacks of ceramic tiles.

"I've never been in here," Brenda said, her tone both wondering and uneasy. Taking advantage of her distraction, Gauther flipped the outside lock on the door and closed it, locking them in. The chatter of passing students was instantly sealed off, plunging the room into an eerie silence.

"Is this really necessary?" Brenda asked in a small, fragile voice amidst the chaos. She forced a smile that did a poor job of masking her unease. "I mean, I don't want to let my friends down. I promised I'd spend time with them."

"Friends can wait," he replied, his left hand buried deep in his pocket, fingers caressing the cold metal of the necklace resting there. "Your education is what truly matters."

Brenda's eyes darted around the cluttered space, taking in the overturned chairs and paint-splattered tarps. Gauther took a step forward. He reached out his right hand to cup her cheek. His thumb brushed over her skin like a lover's caress.

"So perfect," he murmured, his voice barely audible as it floated through the air between them. "Just like a doll."

She flinched away from his touch. "I need to go," she whispered, turning toward the locked door. She fumbled with the door, trying to open it. It rattled back and forth but remained stubbornly shut.

"If this is a joke, Professor Gauther, it's not funny." Her voice was high and tense, growing more frantic by the second. Panic was setting in, and she would start screaming if Gauther didn't deal with her soon.

Patient as a winter's dawn, Gauther pulled a necklace from his pocket and took a step forward. While Brenda was frantically rattling the door, he looped the necklace around her neck and pulled it tight.

"My name is not Gauther," he whispered, his breath a loving caress on her neck as he leaned back, lifting her off the ground. "It's Gray. Byron Gray."

NOW AVAILABLE!

SOMEWHERE WHOLE
(A Piper Woods FBI Suspense Thriller—Book Three)

Former FBI Special Agent Piper Woods, expert tracker and survivalist, left the force behind after a traumatizing case to live far off the grid. But an elusive killer is at work deep in the Everglades, in terrain so hostile that only Piper stands a chance at saving the next victim time…

"Molly Black has written a taut thriller that will keep you on the edge of your seat… I absolutely loved this book and can't wait to read the next book in the series!"
—Reader review for Girl One: Murder

SOMEWHERE WHOLE is book #3 in a long anticipated new series by critically-acclaimed and #1 bestselling mystery and suspense author Molly Black, whose books have received over 2,000 five-star reviews and ratings.

A page-turning and harrowing crime thriller featuring a brilliant and tortured FBI agent, the Piper Woods series is a riveting mystery, packed with non-stop action, suspense, twists and turns, revelations, and driven by a breakneck pace that will keep you flipping pages late into the night. Fans of Rachel Caine, Teresa Driscoll and Robert Dugoni are sure to fall in love.

Future books in the series are also available.

"I binge read this book. It hooked me in and didn't stop till the last few pages… I look forward to reading more!"
—Reader review for Found You

“I loved this book! Fast-paced plot, great characters and interesting insights into investigating cold cases. I can't wait to read the next book!”
—Reader review for Girl One: Murder

“Very good book… You will feel like you are right there looking for the kidnapper! I know I will be reading more in this series!”
—Reader review for Girl One: Murder

“This is a very well written book and holds your interest from page 1… Definitely looking forward to reading the next one in the series, and hopefully others as well!”
—Reader review for Girl One: Murder

“Wow, I cannot wait for the next in this series. Starts with a bang and just keeps going.”
—Reader review for Girl One: Murder

“Well written book with a great plot, one that will keep you up at night. A page turner!”
—Reader review for Girl One: Murder

“A great suspense that keeps you reading… can't wait for the next in this series!”
—Reader review for Found You

“Sooo soo good! There are a few unforeseen twists… I binge read this like I binge watch Netflix. It just sucks you in.”
—Reader review for Found You

Molly Black

Bestselling author Molly Black is author of the MAYA GRAY FBI suspense thriller series, comprising nine books (and counting); of the RYLIE WOLF FBI suspense thriller series, comprising six books; of the TAYLOR SAGE FBI suspense thriller series, comprising eight books; of the KATIE WINTER FBI suspense thriller series, comprising eleven books (and counting); of the RUBY HUNTER FBI suspense thriller series, comprising five books (and counting); of the CAITLIN DARE FBI suspense thriller series, comprising six books (and counting); of the REESE LINK mystery series, comprising six books (and counting); of the CLAIRE KING FBI suspense thriller series, comprising five books (and counting); and of the PIPER WOODS mystery series, comprising five books (and counting).

An avid reader and lifelong fan of the mystery and thriller genres, Molly loves to hear from you, so please feel free to visit www.mollyblackauthor.com to learn more and stay in touch.

BOOKS BY MOLLY BLACK

PIPER WOODS FBI SUSPENSE THRILLER
SOMEWHERE SAFE (Book #1)
SOMEWHERE SANE (Book #2)
SOMEWHERE WHOLE (Book #3)
SOMEWHERE FAR (Book #4)
SOMEWHERE WRONG (Book #5)

CAITLIN DARE FBI SUSPENSE THRILLER
COME GET ME (Book #1)
COME FIND ME (Book #2)
COME TAKE ME (Book #3)
COME CATCH ME (Book #4)
COME SAVE ME (Book #5)
COME STOP ME (Book #6)

MAYA GRAY MYSTERY SERIES
GIRL ONE: MURDER (Book #1)
GIRL TWO: TAKEN (Book #2)
GIRL THREE: TRAPPED (Book #3)
GIRL FOUR: LURED (Book #4)
GIRL FIVE: BOUND (Book #5)
GIRL SIX: FORSAKEN (Book #6)
GIRL SEVEN: CRAVED (Book #7)
GIRL EIGHT: HUNTED (Book #8)
GIRL NINE: GONE (Book #9)

RYLIE WOLF FBI SUSPENSE THRILLER
FOUND YOU (Book #1)
CAUGHT YOU (Book #2)
SEE YOU (Book #3)
WANT YOU (Book #4)
TAKE YOU (Book #5)

DARE YOU (Book #6)

TAYLOR SAGE FBI SUSPENSE THRILLER

DON'T LOOK (Book #1)
DON'T BREATHE (Book #2)
DON'T RUN (Book #3)
DON'T FLINCH (Book #4)
DON'T REMEMBER (Book #5)
DON'T TELL (Book #6)

KATIE WINTER FBI SUSPENSE THRILLER

SAVE ME (Book #1)
REACH ME (Book #2)
HIDE ME (Book #3)
BELIEVE ME (Book #4)
HELP ME (Book #5)
FORGET ME (Book #6)
HOLD ME (Book #7)
PROTECT ME (Book #8)
REMEMBER ME (Book #9)
CATCH ME (Book #10)
WATCH ME (Book #11)

RUBY HUNTER FBI SUSPENSE THRILLER

IF I RUN (Book #1)
IF I TELL (Book #2)
IF I LIVE (Book #3)
IF I FORGET (Book #4)
IF I RETURN (Book #5)

CAITLIN DARE FBI SUSPENSE THRILLER

COME GET ME (Book #1)
COME FIND ME (Book #2)
COME TAKE ME (Book #3)
COME CATCH ME (Book #4)
COME SAVE ME (Book #5)

REESE LINK MYSTERY

BEYOND REASON (Book #1)

BEYOND REACH (Book #2)
BEYOND REPAIR (Book #3)
BEYOND DOUBT (Book #4)
BEYOND NORMAL (Book #5)
BEYOND HOPE (Book #6)

Made in the USA
Monee, IL
02 June 2024